J. K. Quinn

Looking Forward

The coming struggle

J. K. Quinn

Looking Forward
The coming struggle

ISBN/EAN: 9783337377489

Printed in Europe, USA, Canada, Australia, Japan

Cover: Foto ©Andreas Hilbeck / pixelio.de

More available books at **www.hansebooks.com**

THE BUTLER CAMPAIGN:

In Massachusetts, 1878.

THE SPRING VALLEY WATERWORKS

The Tramp's March.

The Dedication of the Catholic University, 11th
of November, 1889; Poems, etc.

INSCRIBED TO THE

HEROES OF THE COMING REVOLUTION.

PRINTED BY FRANCIS, VALENTINE & CO.,
SAN FRANCISCO, CAL., 1892.

PREFACE.

GRIEF, hate and fear, doth swell my heart
    with rage;
Man's inhumanity the cause of same.
'Tis not the game of ancient, modern days;
'Tis been the case since prehistoric days.
As age on age arise and centuries roll along,
Revised, renewed, improved the Bible song.
The mighty being that rules countless worlds un-
    known,
Furnished short-hand notes to cunning Jewish
    drones.
In traveling down the river broad of time,
What desolation meets the eye and mind,
Now when an age or solitary day.
But the race been cursed by priests of every shade.
Their present games are loathsome to my mind,
But they all agree to degrade the human kind;
And by their deeds and teachings they're well-known;
For instance Egypt, Erin and New Mexico.
Infallible, the sanctimonious rogues—
Why, yes, of course, it's ever been their boast.
God's chosen folks, they cannot err, 'tis plain;
The Lord's anointed, what a silly game!

Your grip is soft, you'll not much longer stay.
Your flocks are wild, you cannot them reclaim;
They've traveled far and view you now sideways,
And curse the sophistry the world enchains.
The mighty branches of the great white race,
All came from Asia at the various dates;
Games obsolete seven thousand years ago,
Renewed, revamp'd, rehashed as Bible notes.
As Diana's temple in prehistoric Greece,
Your classical colleges the foul progeny.
You go in as men as the world suppose,
Cursed knaves, fierce monsters, you do come forth.
We've read of Louis, the crusader bold,
That won the heart and hand of Nellie Oge,
The peerless princess of Aquitaine,
A cousin, yes, to our good Pope Adrian;
But Nellie was a little too-too much
On the march to Palestine; she proved it such.
For two years there it was a similar case;
For a monkish king what did the lady care.
With much feigned grief the Pope did them remate,
To Henry II gave the queen of Aquitaine.
For the good King Lewis he did next provide,
Gave him the peerless Constance for his royal bride.
Which go to prove that kings and holy popes,
Away above all sin, and foul reproach;
They cannot err, no matter what their crimes,
E'en though cannibals, with the gang all right.

Looking Forward.

TIME 1895.

SCENE—*The Banks of the Rhine—Republican Camp.*

LOVE, hope and joy my spirits animate
On beholding freedom in her regal state.
Oh, long the night, but now, thank God, the
day,
That hand to hand, the cursed tyrants quake.
The joyous laugh no more proclaims the fact
That royalty, this day, is on a lark.
All sorts of cads doth tremble on this day;
Their palsied hearts doth fear for church and state.

[*The Curtain goes up and discovers leading members of
the Dreibund in Council.*]

THE ITALIAN COUNT CAPRIVANI.

Oh, vast, portentous, this uprising great;
Momentous, too, with cares of Church and State.
As wont we now the rabble can't ignore,

As points to-day of vantage they have scor'd
At noon to-day I met a general bold,
And freedom's colors such he proudly wore;
He, the friend, companion, of my boyish days;
But the wine and oil don't blend upon this day.

Just as of yore, I took the hero's hand— *
Proud his bearing, his the manly grasp;
Saying, Grogan, I had never thought it so,
That you would part with friends of long ago.
I would just soon think of earth giving up its dead,
Or old Mother Ocean leave its present bed,
Or the sea, itself, become solidified,
As you to forsake your race and noble line.

The Revolution gain'd some points, I own.
As the bee to summer, short indeed the score;
As the spring freshet, that some damage makes
The coming crop, fully amends the same.
As all Nature's elements, so social life,
And this day's gloom came of to-morrow's joy.
So the revolution—a cyclone to-day,
A calm to-morrow, to be brush'd away.

GROGAN.
It's a reign of terror since Cæsar's day;

And living or dead, how low the common clay.
For the classes all and everything is right,
And grief and woe the masses sure betide.
This class legislation, this grading stock,
A blasphemy, should be the work of God;
Your classical institutions without a hoax,
A mighty stink from them to heaven doth soar.
The time is come, none dare the point gainsay;
The crop is ripe, an odor from the same.

Your propping, bolstering, so flimsy known,
The miracle racket is thrown overboard.
Where's your supports upon this blessed day?
Your recruiting grounds, all of the past 'tis plain;
Italy, Spain, old Erin just the same,
The sons of freedom that are known there.
Awakened thoughts your work to crush 'tis plain;
You put men to death for uttering of the same.
The laws of science, reason, you ever crush;
The light of day, for you, it is too much.
You put men to death for saying the world is round;
You, steeped in ignorance the most profound.

It was Irish scholars that taught Charlemagne,
And he rehearsed it to the Pope, the case.

Strasburg fell a week ago today;
You claim that Lucifer again prevailed,
And if it's so it simply shows the fact
That a myth, a fable is your venal god.
Cologne will fall before another week,
Despite the vaunting power of Germany;
As the rushing tide, or mountain torrent's roar,
Fair freedom's sons prevail all o'er the globe.

CAPRIVANI.

As the solar system, so on earth God's ways;
'Cept God all subject to blot and stain.
All men can err, we dare not to refute,
And retribution it is ever due.
This a purification, and nothing more,
And the Lord of all will Church and State support.
Men born free and equal, it we do ignore;
It's never so, nor will till time's no more.

GROGAN.

Measures of capacity are men we claim,
All held responsible for what they contain,
But the starved cayuse of our mountain wilds
For the mighty race-horse no match we find.
Where you're in power, the statement's true and fair,

Fierce cunning knaves, are those that hold the
    reins;
And nature's noblemen, the true and brave,
You goad to death, consign to early graves.
Your history in Italy and Spain,
And young folks' history of France the same.
A straightforward story the whole contains,
And religion, your 'butments sure are weak.
Poor fervid Erin, we cannot pass you by;
You, a strumpet old, by Church and State we find.
Of course the work of cunning Church and State—
As the wolf and fox, they ever hold the reins.

CAPRIVANI.

I won't accept and yet I can't refute;
A shade there may be somewhere of the truth.
But this great uprising of such vast import,
Is but chaos, anarchy, and nothing more.
Since dawn of day, since infancy of time,
The mobs were wrong and never will be right.
As the ocean's fury on a rock-bound coast,
A calm soon follows the mob's wild uproar.
Then shall our monks and Jesuits all return,
And holy incense on our altars burn;

Then shall our friars white and abbots gray
With our bishops, cardinals, in regal state.
Strasburg will be built in imperial state.
It, the seat of empire of Charlemagne,
As fit seat of empire Cologne again shall raise,
With its mighty watch-towers o'er the million slaves.

[*Scene changes to the Republican Camp. Characters,* BAR-
ON DE PALM, GENERAL NIERWENDEN, AND COL. LEFLER,
are sitting in council. They rise and come forward.]

DE PALM.

Secure, my friends, upon the open plain—
It is much safer than a fortress great.
Those demons, monsters of the azure wastes,
The mighty fortress their wished-for game.
Your cannons planted as ne'er before,
And pointed vertical, a game ne'er known—
The hawks or demons of the azure wastes
You bring them down, as huntsman does his game.
The demons are best stock of Church and State.
You, the dread avengers of the human race—
To evade your guns, their flight must be so high
That friends and foes to them will be alike.
No doubt whatever the attempt they'll try;
But here they'll fail—on that I bet my life.

NIERWENDEN.

My honor'd friend, thrice welcome to our side!
We fear'd that you with church and state might bide.
There are others, too, of proud and noble race—
With such as these, we're victors in the game.
And from a scout's ascent upon last night,
We learn'd our foes, their distance fifty miles.
Their hosts are mighty as the mighty sea.
Still, a thrill of terror through the whole doth creep.

The imperial jacket and the colors gay,
The grand harangue from officers of state,
The evolutions, drillings, and gay parades,
They lack in spirit, as in by-gone days.
The prayers, benedictions, of monks and saints,
The holy bishops an impress to make,
The whispering zephyr to the stormy gale.
The feudal games availeth not to-day.

Two famous officers are on our side;
As well to say three-fourths of rank and file,
And their love is turned to intense hate,
For who, of course, but those of Church and State?
A horse to water you can easily lead,
But he won't drink, when of it there's no need.

Those vast battalions, those armies great,
Their weight how cumbersome to Church and State.

LEFLER.

The mighty Herman in days of yore,
The Augean stables he cleaned out in Rome—
He ousted Pope and cardinals besides,
He installed a Pope and cardinals likewise.
Affairs of Rome, how rotten in that age,
A genuine type of Alaric's, Attila's days.
Though Vandals call'd, the name is no disgrace,
And praise forever unto Herman's name.

The sons of Herman, in fam'd Otto's days,
To Rome they marched to straighten things again;
Where three maiden virgins for two hundred years,
The man that pleased them, was the Pope indeed.
But Otto came, and with his victorious host
He flogged and scourged, and threw them over-
      board;
He called an election to elect a Pope;
From then till now, the custom's been in vogue.

Martin Luther, a son of Herman bold,
A good holy man, on business went to Rome.
To the Holy City he the closer came,

The less of religion—it vanished in air.
In the Sacred Senate! in the name what gall!
A fierce gang of ruffians, both one and all.
Saying, " Could I from Rome this time but get away,
Nought could induce me to return again.

With King John of Saxony he a refuge found;
His writings then from lethargy aroused.
The millions listened to his noble call,
And reform followed, a great balm for all.
From reform followed able-bodied christianity;
Then rape, rapine, war, at one stretch, thirty years.
But reform rotten as the parent stock—
A blasphemy, the whole that must be smashed.

The Moor, the Turk, and Algerine, also;
Acres of wives these mighty men can boast.
They got the power from God—they frankly own
Their title good; the tripod stands alone.
With them, indeed, there is no forbidden fruit.
The long-possession title none dispute;
Their centuries' wars; theirs no empty boast—
Neither Jew nor Christian o'er them can soar.

The Czar, the Kaiser, and King, also,
They got the power from high, they proudly boast—

Our Holy Father, the Blessed Pope;
A good square set the even number four.
Of course the gang on one great point agree,
That the human race, the best of property.
Ignorance and religion, their stock in trade
To hold them down, the million millions slaves.

Arouse once more from lethargy,
Brave sons of Herman great,
From the Baltic Sea to Ebro's wave,
Fair Freedom, that appeals—
The free and bold, the hearts of oak,
That the Pope and King discard.
As the lightning's blast, our battle shock;
Great Herman's shade that talks.

The American Republic
O'ershades the earth well-known,
And yet but in its infancy.
A hundred years ago—
Not of kingdoms overturned,
Not of empires overthrown—
Three millions of inhabitants
About the whole composed.

Who fears to speak of kingly knaves,

Much less the holy Pope?
The day's long passed when we feared the cads,
The knaves of Kings and Popes.
Brothers awake! fair freedom speaks—
Down, down, with those knaves and drones!
For the classic halls, the palace walls,
The Church and State must go!

From Cæsar's reign until this day,
Affairs about the same;
The government makes a big grand sweep,
The Church takes what remains.
With insults galore, from cads and blokes,
We can't do naught but grieve.
Long ripe the fruit; and tyranny's doom'd—
Long the scourge of earth you've been.

The reformation gave some light,
The more to aggrieve the pain;
The revolution in sunny France
Our grief somewhat assuaged.
But from Venice banks to Baltic sands,
The despots rule the same;
And the light's too strong; the masks are off;
From here you'll pull your freight.

[*A scene in the Palace of Munich—Headquarters of the
Royal Army.   Characters,* EMPERORS FRANCIS JOSEPH,
WILLIAM, KING HUMBERT, FIELD MARSHALS, ETC., ETC.]

JOSEPH.

Dear Brother Willie, your presence here
Doth fill with joy my much declining years.
Oh! this a day of dread and wild alarms,
As though Pandemonium was up in arms!
Whoe'er could dream, or even think or tell
Of this mighty muster of the low canaille.
Strasburg's fall it grieved my heart full sore,
And fam'd Cologne it grieved me ten times more.
Our favorite Hawk return'd from a cruise;
The dreaded news, it does me sore confuse.
Alsace and Lorraine are covered o'er
With armies, such as never seen before.
The panoply of the war of other days
The whole are vanished from the scenes to-day.
French officers that's mostly in command,
And Germans too doth give a helping hand;
And Americans a few were surely seen—
What they don't know, no use for in those scenes.
Their camps so strange, to those some time ago;
Their tactics too, not heard of e'er before;

The quiet in camp most strange of all was seen,
As though mighty monsters had lain asleep.
At sights so strange, my scouts were sorely puzzled,
As though another era had dawn'd upon the world.
But cavalry it cuts no figure there.
There are no Hawks to plow the azure wastes;
They're raw recruits, not much inured to war,
And first success doth count for nought at all.
'Tis true their hearts are centered in the cause,
And that amends for much may be at fault.
'Tis true their hatred of Church and State
Doth nerve their hearts as incarnate fiends to-day.
By silent teachers they have been taught,
And dread avengers we'll find them all;
And come what will, upon next battle-day
There will be no quarter given, or ta'en, 'tis plain.

EMPEROR WILLIAM.

Sire, calm your grief, please do not be dismay'd;
To-morrow's sun will find our troops array'd.
Our armies are so strong upon this day,
The tide alone their mighty march could stay.
Italy, Austria and Germany,
The powers of earth could never make them yield.

Our hawks shall drop their desolating hail.
The rebs shall fly in terror and dismay;
Our cavalry shall charge them, sword in hand,
Nor quarter give not while a man doth stand.
Their army now this side the river Rhine,
Our force in front, the mighty trap behind;
Our cavalry to it refer again.
Since the world began, there's naught to it compares.
A hundred thousand a close estimate,
A dreadful carnage we anticipate;
And when our Hawks let drop their fiery hail,
The terror of hell their army will pervade.
What can they do 'gainst demons of the air?
They'll fall as flies beneath the polar wave.
Then our dragoons with Austria's hussars,
Shall complete the work and terminate their fall.
It is most perplexing, it is vexing too,
That our slaves and chattels would annoy! confuse.
And the Little Father of the Russians great
The people's ally—what a picture strange,

[*Enter* FIELD MARSHAL MANTEUFFEL.]

MANTEUFFEL.

Sires, in compliance with your high command,

The plan of battle unto you I've brought.
Upon the north we do them outflank.
Should emergency or action so demand,
We've pontoon bridges right close at hand,
And in short time the mighty Rhine we span—
Not of the flimsy style of days long gone,
But a whole division can get on at once.
Our center lines, how strong I can't explain,
But there's naught on record to the same compares.
And should our lines through strategy fall back,
The enemy would surely be entrapped.

Now, a new departure in all details,
And our plan of battle to the same compares.
For situation not a plat of ground
O'er Europe broad this day can now be found.
Our guns are planted, such size and shape,
And their supports are guns of greater range.
Their army now's upon this side of Rhine,
And there will stay—on this I pledge my life.
They may get back the point, I won't gainsay,
But through our lines they'll never force their way.
Our men and officers, honest, frank, and fair;
And treachery—of it not yet complaint.

[*Enter the Austrian Field Marshal*, NUGENT.]

NUGENT.

In obedience to my Sire's decree,
I brought plan of battle, points of strategy.
A million marshal'd to play their parts.
The human race, this day it stands appall'd.
Our cannons, too, I think they well might vie
With those of friends or foes on either side.
Our cavalry, should our foes but be confused,
Then what dread, what terror, in the interlude!
Our points of 'vantage we have many scor'd,
And naught on earth this day our lines can force.
The mighty demons of the azure wastes—
They might disrupt us—the case is plain;
But hand to hand, and physical forces try,
As well assail the mighty walls of Troy.
Our Hawk's returned from an extended cruise.
The bonny bird is pleased with all the news.
In Russia the Nihilists all dead to-day,
The Little Father and the people great;
The Turk, proud and arrogant as long ago,
And with the Dreibund he's in heart and soul.
This day he's pleased with Christianity,
And that Christ and Mahomet would allies be.

The revolutionists he loathes, abhors;
He swears Christ and Mahomet must rule all o'er all.

The news from Spain this day is very mix'd.
They're mighty enemies of the infant King,
Yet royalty there still doth hold the reins,
And sullen quiet the order of the day.
Should outbreak come, the facts we can't suppress,
The revolution would come out first best.
In royalty, this day, there's no relax—
How arrogant with colors nail'd to mast,
The dukes and grandees ever fierce and bold.
The dons and donnas play same bugle note;
The sullen silence, cause of much alarm—
The true index of the coming storm.
The're corrupt statesmen, the churchmen mask'd,
The cause of rebound, as the boomerang.
There fierce the unity of Church and State,
The strengthened lines, way down to lowest grade;
The laws of science on the present day
To the masses gives full and complete sway.
'Tis fear'd by all when comes the dreaded day,
The earth itself, in terror then will quake.
Then Portugal will simply follow suit,
And, as in Spain, one deal the pair will do.

O'er Norway, Sweden and Denmark, too,
We spent two days in gathering up the news.
The fierce, bold spirit of days long gone by,
In Scandinavia none to-day we find.
Two-thirds are monarchists, and no mistake;
The remaining third doth quietly hug their chains
Yet the foreign legion in the people's van,
All Scandinavians, twenty thousand strong,
Grand and imposing, strong and bold of heart—
A Swedish prince the same to-day commands.

In the British Isles a few hours we remained;
As yet the Britons rule the rolling main;
But the noise, commotion, and horrid din,
Proclaim the fact that lawlessness commenced.
England cannot spare a man to-day
In aid of Pope, or royal kingly state.
Her force at home, in much demand the case;
There, Royalty a trembling reed to-day.
Just as in Spain, much sullenness prevails,
With every town and every house prepared
The electric spark, so utilized today.
The country folks, the whole they can explain;
Nought to prevent a fanatic or knave
To sweep the land, as polar blast the plains.

All, all alarmed, and all are much afraid,
And that's the cause of lawlessness today.

[*The Italian General*, ORLANDA.]

ORLANDA.

With a half a million men I come to aid
The holy Pope, and royal kingly state;
Fully equipped, it is no silly boast,
With an equal number to hold our own.
Our cavalry is thirty thousand strong,
To strengthen, guard, the passes on left flank;
Our arms, equipment in every line,
To suit the genius of the present times;
Our reserves at home fully two millions strong;
More than enough to dare the power of France.
Our fleet, as yet, has had no work, we own,
But the Mediterranean it can clear of foes.
Our flying demons through the air doth go;
Our torpedo boats the ocean's depths explore;
But a chill, a tremor, is felt everywhere,
And frightful wrongs are whispered through the air.
Aeriel ships 'tis claimed that France got none,
And Russia, too, nought in that line can boast;
But our astronomer on yestereen
Hath seen a scene that blanched his cheeks with fear.

With glass in hand, by accident, he saw
A sight in air which did his heart appall—
An aerial ship, her lines bespoke her French.
They must have more than one, we surely think.

An eastward view to his horror soon disclosed
Another ship, and westward she was going.
The double eagle she did disport,
And the polar bear her nation now disclose.
They met and compliments they did exchange,
As our ocean ships on the rolling main
In their native element eagles not more—
Than those aerial cruisers of which I've spoke.

No affiliation upon this day,
Between the officers and men, 'tis plain;
But as overseers to the lowly slave.
Such days are gone, our soldiers men today.
Freedom now, it is the mighty game,
And sympathy all classes doth pervade.
A nation's boundaries does not debar
The call to freedom in this dreaded war.

[*Scene in one of the Hohenzollern Castles in Suabia. Enter*
AMBASSADOR *from the Republican Camp, escorted by
the Royal Guards.*

AMBASSADOR.

This an honor I ne'er sought,
With danger it may well be fraught;
To play my part, it well behooves
All graceful airs and nothing rude.
My part is difficult to play;
Small experience in that way.
Of princely life, oh, what I know
I've read in books, and nothing more.
Their escutcheons and heraldry,
Republicanism at would sneer;
Their bearing high, and royal airs,
Republicanism at would stare;
But business, when it comes to that,
I'll hold my own whate'er the cost.
Lines are drawn that I must follow
This very night or on to-morrow.
The work, it is too serious far,
Though spirit and soul are in the task.

[*Enters an* ATTENDANT, *who salutes our* AMBASSADOR *in the
free and easy grace of a German of high rank.*]

ATTENDANT.

Your presence here it doth much please,
Your bearing high and manly grace;

And inmates here, at present few,
You won their hearts as you passed through.
You, unaccustomed to our ways.
No doubt, you, from a distant state,
Should you permit, will introduce
Unto our John, the present duke;
Unto his family, also,
The few that's in this once stronghold—
The stronghold of the long ago.
Slim shelter now it does afford,
So changed the modes of cruel war;
To hide away, no chance at all.
Your card the business doth explain;
Your name and rank proclaims the same;
But French, American, what you be,
Of that I'd speak to family.

AMBASSADOR.

An American, I, of ancient British race,
And Charles Herndon is my lawful name.
A Republican by inheritance I claim,
Since Britain trod by Cæsar's legions there.
Republicanism, Celtic inheritance,
For that our race went into banishment.
Ay, even yet in those ancient days

We preferr'd Erin to being Roman slaves.
In Erin still our race doth flourish there—
The name though changed, the stock is all the same.
On the restoration, in King Charles's days,
As to-day, the Church and State we could not bear.
The good Mayflower, yes, and Plymouth Rock,
New England's snows, proclaim our race and stock.
In the revolution, on land and sea,
The gap of danger suits our family.
In eighteen and twelve on the coast of Spain,
Impressed in history our simple name,
In war with Moors and cursed Algerines;
Since then the pirate brood has gone to sleep.
Our favorite element, the ocean spray,
And green the memory of our action there.
When this war broke out, I was sec. to Minister Reid,
So I joined this army as a volunteer.
And come what will, a friend in me you'll find,
Though with my instructions I must comply.

[*Enter the* GRAND DUKE JOHN ROMUALDO HOHENZOLLERN.
etc., accompanied by the GRAND LADY DOWAGER, *etc.,
and daughters* FLORENTINA, JOSEPHINA, *etc. The
manly grasp of the Duke, as well as the tender clasp of
the ladies, was quite enjoyable by our hero.*]

DUKE.

My noble friend, a thousand welcomes here,
But as your mission has preceded thee,
To talk on business we now refrain·—
A dreary subject, that gives much pain.
You must be weary and hungry;
Then please accept our hospitality.
When you're refreshed and nature's wants appeased,
Our best regards will send you quite to sleep.

The meal being o'er, and in the parlor grand
The music veil'd.   As though in fairyland,
This lovely maiden of a royal race
Then took his hand; a waltz that now was play'd.
Oh what a scene, now of happiness.
A lovely picture of terrestrial bliss.
And war so dread, with its dire alarms,
Forgotten now in love and lady's charms.

The chamber where our hero lay,
Was grand, resplendent in a way.
For here the bust of Charlemagne,
And Charles Martel's of great fame.
The Emperor Otto's too is there.
The hero of heroes, in his day.

Here Cross and Crescent too displayed
The frightful wars of Crusade age.
Here trophies of the field and chase,
A ducal chamber, sure they grace.
Here battle scenes of days gone by,
From Alaric's day to present time.
The great Lord Clare here once confined,
In this strong hold of feudal times;
His picture, too, on Blenheim's day;
At Fontenoy 'tis also there,
The pictures are presum'd to please
The stray-aways from other states.
The chamber of the son and heir,
In royal camp a general there.
My attendant usher, a nobleman,
Of easy grace, and manners bland.
He fill'd a glass of Suabian wine—
His toast our flag, my health likewise.
To me a glass he next pour'd out,
Saying not a word, but drink it down.
He filled again, saying, 'Tis our wish
Your happy rest, your sleep of bliss.

The wild excitement of the day,
Good wine and sleep, doth banish care.

Of short duration was his sleep—
He's raving incoherently;
Of war and love his fevered dreams,
New England home, United States,
His Dragon sailing through the air,
The peerless princess that she bears.

His dream's again of human race,
The monsters that degrade the same;
Man's inhumanity to man
Since civilization first began;
Of battle-fields and cruel wars,
The greatest leveler of them all;
Of Minister Reid, good and great,
The most admir'd and fear'd to-day.

Of beauteous princess now he dreams,
Of line of mighty Charlemagne.
What condescension on their part!
"And fear the prompter of the acts."
For her, indeed, he'd sacrifice
Of Rocky Mountains quite a slice.
'Long Chesapeake bay or Hudson side
A home for all he would provide.

"Minister Reid must see me through;

The compliments are overdue.
Our glorious flag, its ample folds
Enough for to protect the whole.
Should I but win the princess fair,
And noble brands from fire to save,
Good-by, adieu, to worldly care,
In our pleasant home on Hudson stream."

No rest in bed our hero finds,
With thoughts of war and love likewise.
Adventures all on land and sea,
This one a thousand such exceeds.
To up and dress one minute takes,
And o'er the ground he promenades,
And mighty Mars takes holiday,
For Venus surely leads the way.

As Aurora merging from ocean's deep,
Or the Queen of Heaven, in terrestrial sleep,
Or the Queen of Beauty on Ida's hill.
Our peerless princess approaching him—
The pride of Nature, this glorious being,
Not e'er before her equal he had seen.
With kindling eye, with loving, tender clasp:
"My father comes, give news, the best you can."

Lord John Romualda Rehonda Hohenzollern, etc.

Your buoyant step, your pleasant, cheerful face,
Proclaims the fact your mind is free from care;
I hope your sleep with appearances comport;
So come inside, the news, I want to know."
A package of letters, a good round score,
Unto the lord our Charley handed forth.
He viewed the whole, and then burst into tears,
Saying, "The royal Bourbon sends greetings here."

Letters from friends of a by-gone age,
And from brothers in arms of other days.
Letters from officers of high degree,
Though tied by cause are still in sympathy.
A Nation's greeting sends Minister Reid,
And a field marshal, the great O'Neil;
But the one of sorrow, mix'd with worldly care,
From the Royal Bourbon, the presumptive heir.

The Dispatch.

" Cousin and friend, of the present I would write,
Of the mighty issues that distract my mind.
Since time began, since civilization's dawn,
These present issues doth o'ershade them all.
The people *en masse* the whole affiliate;

And grief and woe betide the Church and State.
Such mighty armies ne'er dreamt of before—
Millions now, where thousands as of yore—
Such destruction, havoc, and slaughter great;
And still no fighting, it seems so strange.
Two weeks ago, upon this very day,
Dispatch to Strasburg—'Surrender, right away,
Or in ten hours our armies will begin,
And naught can stay destruction when commenced.'

''A royal army garrison'd the place,
The Republicans were twenty miles away.
'Twas but a joke, the Royalists had claim'd;
The moment, hour, proclaimed no joke was there;
At 11 P. M., appointed moment, time,
As though the mountains belching smoke and fire,
As though earthquakes and chasms into life had
    sprung,
And destroying angels claim'd our race was run.
In fifteen minutes, since the storm began,
And Strasburg's ruins, describe them now who can.
The agencies on Strasburg brought to bear,
As though product of earth, heaven, hell and air.
''How calm the night, how beautiful the scene,
Yet not a man of storming party seen.

From whence they came, the wonder where they're
    gone,
As though earth had swallowed up the warlike
    throng;
As though invisible beings of the azure wastes
Had reproduced Gomorrah on a latter day.
One mighty fact to deduce from case,
The royal armies will not prevail.

" The royal troops an advantage gained;
What fearful slaughter in short time they made;
A fierce reaction, a dread rebound,
As hay in June, the Royalists strewn around.
That's why Cologne had met a similar fate;
The fates, the gods, array'd 'gainst Church and State;
Their armies apparently as tidal waves,
As the summer flies about as they prevail."

'Tis the feudalism of the ages gone,
By brutal power and tyranny such back'd;
Cursed ignorance taught by classical drones,
'Gainst the laws of science; what impotent force,
Mighty power, from kings doth emanate.
From the people comes the mighty power to day;
To the foreign pastures the flocks have stray'd,
And with the flocks 'tis best to emigrate.

Count our force, as the leaves of forest wide
Estimate our power, as the rise and fall of tide.
Though all our men this day into atoms blown,
By next full moon, another army grown—
Were we bent on slaughter as the Royal force,
We'd soon lay out all, all opposing force;
No silly talk, no idle vaunting boasts,
In a week we'd slay the armies of the globe.

You have friends here, a few that's high in place,
Of lineage high and old and kingly race.
When Roman glory began to wane,
All over Europe their banners blaz'd;
Their kingly power for centuries passed, I ween;
But still they're prominent in other fields—
To wield the sword, the truncheon or the shield,
And to sit in council, 'mongst the highest be.

Amongst the number, I one approached,
And touched upon the thousand griefs and woes;
Amongst the many I mentioned yours,
Which pal'd his cheeks; he look'd somewhat con-
    fused.
" A debt of gratitude to his race we owe,
And with God's help we'll square accounts, I hope;

Though old the debt, 'tis not too late to pay,
But short, the time there is none now to spare."

O'NEILL.

To Minister Reid, upon this day,
And to him I'll explain the case;
If in his power, he'll grant my boon,
To save Lord John from utter ruin;
A debt of gratitude we owe.
The debt is old, thrown out of court;
But debts of honor never old—
We'd pay the bill one hundred fold.

REID.

The orders from United States:
All social rents to regulate;
To scatter oil upon the storm,
And good to all in lieu of harm;
To do a favor when a chance,
And then no crime or blame attach'd;
And before I'd refuse O'Neill,
I'd run the risk incurring blame.

To hoist our flag on Linden Hall—
No wrong in case, no cause of jar,
No batteries mask'd, no trap prepar'd—

A common free zone.   On to-day
Charles Herndon, without delay;
Commissioned for a year to stay,
To hoist our flag on Linden Hall,
In proud defiance of them all.

Herndon is a nervy man,
That's bold of heart and free to act.
The stars and stripes from tower will float,
And Linden castle we will hold.
You get John from there away,
Into your camp, without delay,
And foes and friends will be amazed
At stars and stripes in highest place.

A council now our inmates call'd—
Lord John, the Usher, dame and all.
It was agreed the Lord should leave,
And take the Usher too away;
Our hero to be left in charge,
To raise the glorious stripes and stars,
And foes and friends the whole stand off,
Till time is ripe for to unmask.

Lord John and Usher, gone away,
As best they can to find their way;

3

To seek the friends of other days,
And try all games to save the place,
His grand excuse to visit Reid,
And royalty no passport needs.
His lovely wife, and daughter fair,
Nephew young, menials frail,
And Herndon doth command the place.

Though war is rife this many a day,
It's lesser trouble of our pair;
For Cupid has been playing smash,
With Yankee boy and princess bland.
The fiddle now a servant plays,
As waltz and dance our happy pair.
The lovely dame the scene enjoys,
Its blending of her grief and joy.

His mighty plans to hold the fort,
'Gainst Prussians, French and other foes,
Oh small the odds which gains the day,
The princess grand right here will reign.
His desperate plans he thus imparts,
Smiles with grief the mild response,
But come what will, his nation great
Will regulate the reins of State.

[SCENE—*The Republican Camp.* *Enter* COL. BARRINGTON,
who sings:]
Air—Cove Harbor.

Who talks of kings and kaisers great?
Foul ignorance, their stock in trade;
Cruel powers and brutal force,
Always on top to squeeze the yoke;
And Rome doth furnish wicked knaves
A vasty odor from their games,
The mind and intellect to crush,
Then fluting psalms to saints above.

The missionaries, holy saints,
To hoodoo people, their best game;
The mind and intellect to destroy,
Their game to own all human kind;
To convert first, then next enslave;
The next in order foreign chains.
The soul, the soul, their silly game,
The fool claptrap all gone away.

In prehistoric ages,
We turn our eyes to Greece;
Then mighty Thebes in Egypt—
Earth's focus, all concede.
'Twas kingly power in Egypt,

In Persia, Troy, likewise,
But mighty Greece withstood them all.
The world we then defied.

Jewish history so foul
We will not expatiate.
But good things come from evil—
That's what the Churchmen claim.
But even in their heyday,
They figure rather cheap.
As the buzzards to the eagles,
So the Jews to Greeks compare.

Mighty Rome—no fable—
The offspring of fam'd Greece,
In thought, in word, in deed and fact.
The Gods above were pleased
With Cæsar and Imperialism.
Proud Rome began to wane,
And, blotted from the planet's map,
A filthy stain to-day.

About one hundred years ago,
A republic here in France;
The Pope and kings did then unite
To crush in swaddling bands.

With terror how they eyed the babe.
His growth, how quick and fast!
With palsied hearts they on him gazed,
As rats upon young cats.

With this present mighty struggle
The world itself doth quake.
Church and State all other knaves
'Gainst Republicans array'd.
Coarse, brutal power, foul ignorance
Solidified to-day;
But reason, intellect, and science,
God and Nature will prevail.

[*Scene changes   Enter* COL. WALDINGHAM AND GEN. LIE-
BEG, *couriers from the Royal Camp.*]

It has so pleased their Majesties so great
To send us here you to conciliate.
Their mighty armies, strong as the sea itself,
To cope against there is no power on earth.
Our vasty numbers, by the millions count;
Should you persist, your doom is seal'd no doubt.
Your army here is strong, we have no doubt;
But as mouse to mountain it compares to ours.
A fraction of our force—it is no boast—

Would overwhelm yours, destroy the whole.
Should you withdraw, again recross the Rhine,
A treaty, sure, the Emperor would sign
To their demand; should you but comply,
A peace would follow on which Heaven would smile.
Their majesties on peace now fully bent,
While life remains would surely be your friends.

DANTON.

We feel indebted for their good advice,
With many thanks the offer we decline;
Though all our men should perish in the fray,
And not a soul on soil of France remain,
Though our days became a continuous polar night,
And a glacial era hovering up in sight.
I'll not desist whilst in me lives a soul.
When comes the chance, the treaty, sure, then broke,
Unless they disband their armies now so great,
And submit their power to have them curtail'd.

LIEBEG.

To kingly power the world has long agreed,
And religion essential to harmony.
With late successes you feel elate,
But reverses follow often in their wake.

Is there no hope that we can harmonize
And drag in two the issues that divide?
These jars and brawls can all be thrown aside,
The olives blending with our Rhenish wine.

ROSSENA.

For centuries long the human race been rode;
How long the shank, the rowels were sharp also.
With every age it's still more misery;
There is no change to this sacramental creed.
This royalty it must be brush'd away,
And religion must follow in its wake;
A President as in United States.
It must, it shall, we'll surely make the change.·

WALDINGHAM.

Is this the answer to what I've asked and said?

DANTON.

It is, and bear it back from whence you came.

ROSSENA.

By to-morrow eve a battle there will be,
A dreaded index to the same I've seen.
Sunshine and shadow it casts o'er my mind,
Its interpretation on to-morrow night.
The question to my mind doth now arise:

Do shades of departed ever join in strife?
But one thing certain, a sight on this eve,
The index to defeat or victory.

On looking out an hour ago I spied
Some officers as they were passing by,
In gorgeous dress their apparel gay;
But their conversation I cannot explain.
One tall of stature that surpassed them all;
A demigod, on his breast many a star.
I turned around preparing them to greet,
As though earth had swallow'd, not one to see.

DANTON.

Without a doubt this is the battle eve,
And the glorious harbinger of victory.
The shade of Murat and nothing more.
On the eve of battle he sallies forth;
Wherever seen the lilies gay of France,
Are held aloft and never seem to lag:
Whate'er the cost, victory is assured;
Opponents all he surely doth confuse.

[*Enter an Aerial Courier.*]

At three o'clock, about that time I believe,
An aerial ship hath then appeared to me,

Sailing westward, coming from the east,
And o'er our center as near could be;
Slow her speed, she reconnoitering true
To them portends that we are surely doomed.
Within easy range we could have brought her low;
But against the orders, sô we let her go.

A grand half-circle their mighty line,
Forty-five miles it is from point to point.
On the south they're solidly encamp'd;
In the north they're hustling and curving fast.
Austria and Italy hold the southern lines;
The Prussian blue all o'er the north we find,
Their center strong, compos'd of all we find; ·
Their strength appalling to all human kind.

[*Enter* Liembach, *the Spy.*]

I'm a German by name and race,
And fam'd Alsatia my native place;
Am crippled somewhat, blind of an eye;
But, with the other, many things I spied.
As clown and gambler, 'twas easy work
To pierce their lines by slinging German guff,
And fully ignorant as a spy could be,
'Twas thus I learned of their strategy.

Their left wing immeasurably strong;
It looks as though they intended there to stop.
The strength of center can't so well explain;
But the troops dispirited, and much complain.
Two thirds, at least, Republican at heart,
Will to us fly whene'er the 'ghost of chance.
Our education, through their ranks diffused,
For Church and State they have no further use.

To-morrow morning, by the break of day,
The Prussian troops will then commence the fray.
Double your strength; next your lines they'll break.
To-morrow eve your rout will be complete.
Their left wing next will its lines deploy;
You'll be hemmed in, behind you now the Rhine.
Negotiations all, by now, are thrown aside,
By set of sun Republicanism dies.

But should it pass, you'd stubbornly resist,
And hold the ground, contest it inch by inch,
'Twill prolong the battle until closing eve;
Both sides defeated apparently.
At one o'clock A. M. the dragoons will be here.
Havoc, desolation, will reign supreme.
Such as will escape the carnage then and there—

Oh, soft the snap for cavalry next day.

[DANTON, *handing him a purse of gold, yells:*]
For God's sake, Liembach, give us a rest!

[*Enter a* SCOUT *from the Prussian Army.*]
'Tis great activity in the Prussian ranks.
By to-morrow morning batteries far advanced;
On yonder knoll ten great guns will be placed;
Fifteen miles west, another battery there;
And those field-pieces—not the common sort,
But the greatest batteries ever known before—
Their range how vasty, fully ten good miles;
Their grand supports, just of a similar kind.
Those batteries to shield their grand advance
Retreat to cover, should it come to that,
Their war estimates of a similar sort.
Alone unaided to whip the plebeian hordes,
Their guns will slaughter, us demoralize,
And their mighty cavalry the rest destroy.
[*Aside*] I think different.

DANTON.

In front of first battery, distance eleven miles,
Place Mirabeau, on them to keep an eye.
In front of second battery place Robespierre,

His strict attention to laws of destiny.
And in the center place Murat and staff,
Their glorious shades will warm to the task.
Rifle-pitsmen at each point as well,
And rifles, too, to suit the shades of dead.
With nature's garb, cover best you can.
Oh short the time until comes off the mask.

SCENE— *The Royal Camp.*

MANTEUFFEL.

Our cannons' range doth almost reach their camp;
Our armies now upon them may advance.
Our chiefs, not one, can point to a mistake;
Our plan of battle nought to it compares;
Our numbers count to theirs as three to one;
Our armaments are on a scale most grand.
In the fields of sciences again we lead;
From what I.heard, they follow far in wake;
But the greatest battle that was ever fought,
To this one of Linden will compare as nought.
The greatest issues, since the world began,
Will rise or fall as rise or fall the flags.
Should we fail, then Church and State no more;
All our institutions thrown overboard;

Then a new era on the world would dawn,
With light and reason to govern all.
Then mighty intellects would reign supreme.
We'd have no France, nor neither Germany;
We'd have great States, as in United States,
With a capital somewhere in middle place.
Then farewell the age of monks and flummery,
Then farewell to clergies and to monkeries,
Farewell to white friars and abbots gray,
And to holy penitents in fine array.
The age of miracles will quickly end,
And stern reality will then commence.
Then holy penitents will march no more,
And foolish saints a myth as pagan lore.
Then holy water and whisky straight
Will lose their virtue on election day.
No more will queens and Scotch gillies hide and
    seek,
And the baccarat scandals in harmony.
Then lords and dukes, the spawn of hell, must go,
With their human bloodhounds, causing grief and
    woe.
The grading, degrading, of the human race,
And cursed priests—oh, this their hellish game!

The mighty misery of human race shall cease,
And there will be some semblance of fair play.
What millions live in wretched misery,
And thousands fatten on their poverty.
With Church and State it is a monstrous case.
Their game, the human race to keep enslaved.
The State ennobles them—the case is plain—
By dying on battle-fields, in heaps of slain.
Next, the Church anoints them with all church grace;
There's no switch-off—they go to heaven straight,

DANTON.

At sunrise to-morrow will commence the fray.
Frightful the havoc to contemplate
As though the sun had withdrawn its light,
Or that the day had changed to sudden night,
Or as mighty earthquake, or tidal wave,
This day more frightful to contemplate!
The laws of science have things so prepared,
The die is cast, and science must prevail.
We shall not live—so Church and State doth claim—
But as their property, their chattel slaves.
And who are they, a rotten, leprous horde,
The stink of earth, that made such fulsome boasts?
This royal blood, nauseating to our mind,

Enough to sicken all human kind;
The Holy Church, its cunning priests and monks.
American cities claim they've had enough.
Whatever cause poor human race to bleed,
The Church is rank'd on side of tyranny,
With mighty slave-kings in a by-gone age,
With mighty capitalists upon this day, *
To have the wolf and monkey high in place,
To send impress of divinity to an early grave.
Look at the people under priestly power—
Oh they are 'vangel'd, yes, without a doubt.
Their writings, work, all point to human grief.
This earth they call it the valley of tears.
A poor fallen woman, we of her say
She's what man has made her, it's just the case.
This earth they made it tears and misery.
Their every game, that human nature bleeds.
This earth intended as a heaven for all,
But classical ruffians pervert God's laws.
'Tis for the few a heaven and no mistake—
By you a hell for nine-tenths of the human race.
The Jews have cut a swath, and no mistake;
But foul and dirty their crops of hay.
For many centuries their comings short,

Their doom and curse fulfilled the laws of God.
A word or two about the British Isles:
Without a doubt, an earthly paradise.
England fell beneath the Roman sway,
And Pagan Rome was not as bad as others claimed.
But since Christianity was introduced,
A mighty hell for masses, none dispute.
One God, one Church—what the churchmen claim—
One mighty empire, countless millions slaves!

England's civilization, prior to Hastings' day,
The work of Church, the flocks the churchmen blame.
Cæsar's maxims the priests work to sow,
That is their business and nothing more.
Their civilization just as bad today,
All o'er the globe, where'er they hold the reins.
England's civilization then
Procuring young women, and getting them pregnant,
Bringing them to Ireland, and selling them there.

Ireland's civilization, from the advent of St. Patrick
        till today,
Fighting like devils for a reconciliation,
And hating each other for the pure love of God.
Of the Scottish picture I've naught to say,

Yet it's joint product of the mentioned twain—
That's what historians of Britain claim.

The human race have long been born slaves,
Have grown as such, and yet as such remain;
Ask reason, Nature, should this thing be so?
The very stones with vengeance answer, No!
Their dreaded vows, with desperate vengeance made,
Saying, we'll submit, or they'd exterminate.
But science, Nature, speaks in thunder tones,
That they must go, and reason asks no more.
As three to one, the martial hosts array'd,
As three to one the armaments compare.
Men not born free and equal, of course they claim.
Our men are free, as such they mean to stay.
By to-morrow's eve we will their utmost know;
Should we make a miss, their joy beyond control.
But our pioneer batteries, should they silenced be,
Then Europe broad our vengeance sure would feel.

[*The Royal Camp. Characters,* MANTEUFFEL, WALDING-
HAM AND LIEBEG.

MANTEUFFEL.

Between those batteries will pass our center lines,
To left and right our wings will then deploy;

In numbers, force, by far we doth surpass.
To overwhelm, they'll resist not long.
The news as learned, from our spies and scouts,
They're ill prepared to contest the ground.
They have some guns, that to ours compare;
They are few in numbers, and can't prevail.
Their raw recruits not much inured to storm,
They're stripling youths from school pressed into
    war.
They're careless, impotent, very weak
To compete with ours or cover up retreat.
Upon the ground no point of vantage found;
And just the same for them as 'tis for ours.
No mountain passes, primeval rugged wilds,
Where hundred men against a host might bide.
No overtopping crags, narrow passes underneath.
Cliffs precipitated on armies.
No, here it is a case of physical force,
That's backed by science, the best that's known.
The force of will, superior intellect,
All potent always the world confess.
Another point, all concede the case,
Which e'er best scholar surely gains the day.

[*Half past five, the battle is begun—Long range firing on both sides.*]

The Prussian batteries belching flame and fire,
Between them both advance the royal lines;
A park of artillery in their advance.
The earth it trembles 'neath their cannon's shock.
After one hour's firing the missiles falling short,
From Republicans they fail to get response.
What great commotion in the royal lines,
As to the front their greatest guns they ply.
The firing now doth rend the air and sky.
How the mighty missiles through the air doth fly.
The missiles now doth come so very close,
That Republican troops for miles are lying low.
Mirabeau and Robespierre have fired with care
And true to mark, good center shots are they;
They have fallen short quite a little way,
Still their close proximity a thrill creates.

On the second round the dread effect how great,
A full ten strike each mighty gun had made.
The two royal batteries are silenced now.
In pugilistic parlance two great knockdowns.
Murat and staff are busy, no mistake;
A mighty army they hold at bay.

Good Mirabeau and Robespierre likewise,
Have lent their aid—no advance—retreat we find.

At close of eve how calm all nature seems,
As though a fight or battle ne'er had been.
And scouts are hurrying on land, through air,
To glean all facts of past and coming day.

Two aerial scouts return'd without delay;
Their dread strange mission they both explain.
Great Danton now, with care somewhat confused,
Oh what great attention to the mighty news.

" The Royalists, chagrined at morning duel,
Are bringing to front Krupp's heaviest best im-
    proved,
Directly opposite in line from here,
And but seven miles from our batteries.
Five mighty guns they have laid down with care.
Their work begins about the break of day,
And other batteries they have up in line, •
Much lighter guns of dreaded range we find.
Such speed in moving mighty armaments,
As though the gods were expediting things.
Such fire, such energy, such vim infused,
The news to thee it cannot be too soon."

[*Enter three Generals of the Republican Army.*]

DANTON.

Hail, gallant friend, the news is mighty great,
Momentous to you to communicate:
The royal batteries are coming near,
Within seven miles of Murat and Robespierre,
With you I wish to counsel on the case,
As to your plans; the best one we will take.
Oh! brief the time and short must be the tale.
They're on the march and coming fast this way.
Their thundering cannon will our slumbers scare.

FIRST GENERAL.

Within two hours I can aid Mirabeau,
Make his case good for a month or year I know.

SECOND GENERAL.

And in that time I can reinforce Murat,
Make him, as in life, the dreaded scourge of God.

THIRD GENERAL.

And Robespierre, the glorious silver-tongued,
In flame-tongued tones his thunder notes were
    strung.

DANTON.

By dawn of day we'll hear their cannon play;

Now as to time, how does that suit your case?
"All, all agreed, we're ready for the same."

[*Enter* GENERAL LEFLER, *singing Song of the Battle Ev*

  Long live great Danton! may he reign,
  To curb the pride of Church and State—
  The sons of freedom shout again,
  The glorious revolution!

  Our glorious Hawks, in azure wastes,
  Shall drop their desolating hail;
  This planet they shall desolate—
  Then cheers to the revolution!

  Those leviathans of the deep
  Have long proclaimed our misery;
  Those monsters dread of royalty
  Are doom'd by the revolution!

  At night, when slumbering on the deep,
  Right overhead a Hawk will be,
  That sends them to eternity—
  Then here's to the revolution!

  The steel nets cannot, can't be made
  That can withstand our shears to-day;

Then warships of a by-gone age—
Great change by the revolution.

Thrice welcome to the glorious day
That downs forever Church and State.
They, as suppliant pilgrims, sue for peace
To the glorious revolution.

Chawing the rag, and threshing the air,
Foul relic of despotic age;
The foul *rahmeash* on tap to-day
Gone, gone by the revolution!

The fierce foul work of Church and State,
The dread impressions they have made,
As melts the snow in summer's blaze,
Cleared away by the revolution.

Swill poetry, rhapsodies, that's stale
For low, degraded, hide-bound slaves;
But Freedom's screams, in thunder tones,
Their echoes heard all o'er the globe.

DANTON.

And each of you, independent in command,
On your own judgment each of you must act.

[*The Royal Camp.*]

MANTEUFFEL.

We met some reverses, it we can't deny;
Enough to vex, to tantalize the mind.
Yesterday a set-back, trifling in a way,
It will never mar our glorious joy to-day.
As two to one in front our cannon count,
And three to one our men, without a doubt.
They can't withstand such overwhelming power,
And mid-day's sun will see their complete rout.
The royal orders all are not to spare
A living soul, nor not a prisoner take.
Republican armies all must be destroyed,
Church and State not safe while they're alive.
Republican ideas all must be ignored,
Though blood in rivers over Europe flow'd.
The human race, the whole must be destroy'd,
Or they'll submit to diction from on high.

Just 'twixt the break of day and rising sun,
The mighty battle, it is now begun.
The Royalists, with sudden, sore surprise,
The close proximity of opponents find.
Though molten mountains, into fragments hurl'd,

'hough earthquakes rise which threaten part of
    world.
'hough a tidal wave our seaboard had laid waste,
'he desolation could not be more great.

'he dreaded issues that divide the race,
'hey cannot die while life on earth remains.
.wakened thoughts, that's sent from heaven direct,
.nd utter'd here, they cannot be suppress'd.

'he mighty issues of pagan days,
. myth, a fable, to the present games;
ews, Mohammedans, all else the case,
'heir issues lost, o'ershadowed on to-day.

[o greater issues hath the world e'er known.
['is free or slave, concerns one, the whole.
]ontinued sophism, fogyism of prehistoric days,
)r glorious freedom that's to hold the reins.

'hough Church and State doth reign by divine
    right,
.nd the Supreme Being doth sanction "Might is
    right."
Whatever is, is right, said inspired Pope;
.t's ever so and will, till time's no more,

Through every power that incites will and mind,
No thought so fiendish as ownership of kind,
And such the thoughts that Royalists actuate,
And with Krupp's guns, God's power they'll rein-
  state.

As though Freedom now in robes of glory dress'd,
Direct from regions of the ever bless'd.
As though Mars, and Minerva in radiant sheen,
Inciting Republicans to mighty deeds.
As though the million shades of other days
Were scourging Royalists, now freedom aids.
But every game that mighty minds devise,
All brought to bear, in the dread though glorious
  strife.

The royal batteries, a focus great,
How vast the circle they depopulate;
Fair freedom's cannon not a whit behind—
A circle greater far, they now describe.
Talk of Sharp's or Winchester's improved,
As the old flint lock to rifles now in use.
At the set of sun the combatants withdraw,
But such mighty slaughter the world ne'er saw.

T'was just a draw, the royalists so claim'd—

A dread repulse, if truth was only said.
Not one Republican on battle-field,
But such as those there was the utmost need.
In the royal lines, how thick the squadrons stand,
As though placed there, for destroying angel's hand.
The tactics now, not those of by-gone days;
Now 'tis territory, and each a circle makes.

Kill, kill! the priests did hiss on Hastings' day,
And plenty left for servants, sure the case.
Those Saxons are but filthy common clay,
We God's chosen stock, so Church and State doth
    claim.
Hissing priests then figure small to-day;
God's chosen stock are those that clear the way,
The mighty forces here to utilize.
Tis nature's claim, the people should enjoy.

This mighty sparring for the many years
In regard to which should gain ascendancy.
But the laws of science cannot be controlled
By brutal force as that of kings and popes.
So now the rush to test the knowledge gained.
Procrastination danger would entail.
So, soon array'd to commence again the strife,

The royal center now prepared we find.

The Royalists in crescent shape how strong,
With their mighty batteries in front and flank.
Forty miles in length their dreaded lines,
Irresistible apparently as the ocean tide.
The Republicans' defendants in the case,
An interior line.   Two-thirds its length of space.
Their batteries planted with skill and care,
As though more than man had managed all affairs.

'Tis Rousseau here commands fair Freedom's host
His generals, the world no better knows.
A fighting race fully two thousand years;
Not yet the zenith to their proud career.

Weak in numbers, to them it matters not;
They claim shades of ages to their banners flock.
Change of tactics, now the cards to play—
They adept professors in the mystic game.

At dawn of day, the battle now doth rage;
At closer range, the gunners doth engage.
The scene's indescribable, to say the least;
E'en naught read or dreamt of to it compares;
But science here, as never known before,

And more to-morrow, so knowing ones report—
Oh, dread the issues that such work demands,
Such unrelenting, exterminating war.

All day long, no advance or retreat,
Who gain'd or lost a mystery to this day.
No doubt whatever the slaughter it was great;
Carriers and scouts, both sides, report the same.
The Republicans, most surely, suffered least.
As sentinels, Republican guns were placed,
And gunners protected as never dreamed of before;
And all agree, another victory scor'd!

For several days, from battle now respite,
And vast desertions to fair Freedom's side;
But no desertions, as yet not known,
From Freedom's side to that of Kings and Pope.
What preparations for the final day;
Oh, vast the numbers to be engaged;
But come what will, fair Freedom now prepar'd—
Tis death or victory, but no retreat.

    At dawn of day, all are prepar'd,
    Electric music now that's play'd.
    Again the guns are belching forth
    Much havoc, desolation, woe;

Again our scouts, in azure wastes,
And reconnoitering their game,
On other side the fiery cross,
All must fight, or all is lost.
Death's preparations on this day,
Destroying angels, all are pleased.
With mighty war, its dread engines,
The world, to-day, is paralyzed.
Oh, how all nations quail with fear—
This age of dread and misery.
The issues on this dreaded day
Are other than the route to hades;
And heaven's bliss forgotten here,
This earth the caper, all it yields,
Mourner's bench, penitent's psalms—
The whole are lost, both one and all.
The Ranters with their howls, "the light"—
Yes, e'en the Turks in holy fright,
The Church of Rome in dread alarm,
For all that's out doth breast the storm.
The Czar of all the Russias, too,
The Jews and Nihils he doth pursue.
Fasting, praying, he contemplates
The near approach of latter day.

Young Kaiser Will in bishop's role—
The humor grim, upon my soul!
To die upon the battle-field.
Freedom such he guarantees.
To invoke the aid of holy saints,·
The ever-faithful to them pray.
But, science, all admit the fact,
Will rule the earth, and while it lasts.

Victoria, England's holy queen,
The head of Church—what sanctity!
Whilst pondering on her Scotch gillies,
She's contemplating other scenes:
On holy Irish saints she thinks;
On Parnell, too, with knowing winks;
On Paddy Ford, on Mrs. O'Shea;
Such her litany on this day.

First gentleman of Europe claimed
For the royal sport, the Prince of Wales.
To wear the crown on weekly days,
To steer the Church on Sabbath days—
Why talk of Moses or old Abe,
Great mediators in their day?
As mediator e'en in S——,

Our gallant Prince would all eclipse.

On battle's morning still and calm,
As though all nature seem'd appall'd.
On hill, in vale, no puff of air;
No bird doth sing, no leaf doth shake,
As though all nature seemed fatigued.
This time and place for sleep's embrace—
But hark! the whispering in the air!
Of dread import the meaning same,
And visitors from realms of space,
An index to the mighty game.

The ocean's depths our men explore;
In azure wastes we feel at home.
The science gleaned in present age,
Civilization it doth change.
Miracles of a bygone age,
Silly, simple, old and plagu'd.
The old products must be destroy'd;
The needed room for crops that's ripe.

Just listen to their silly talk,
We're common people, that is all;
Puddle dirt and common clay,
And they're God's chosen, so they claim.

Vaporings, gushings of thousand years
That kept the race in misery.
The monsters dread in human shape,
That sheep doth follow to this day.

Of elements our race we find;
Different are the many minds,
And elements they cannot blend,
Whate'er at first 'tis ever still.
The men that sail through azure wastes
To follow classic monkeys, apes,
Masters of ocean-realms of space,
To follow knaves with shallow brains.

The points of science when obtained
They struggle hard for to obtain:
But the crop of science of to-day
One-tenth they cannot hide away.
Royal dudes and fogy knaves,
No doubt they had a good long reign.
The free, the common red school-house,
The foul false light it has put out.

That is why this mighty war
The world to-day it doth appall.
The subject born on to-day,

4

A subject, yes, while life remains.
Your games are all thrown overboard,
Fair Freedom has them long ignor'd;
Ignorance controll'd by cursed knaves
'Gainst glorious Freedom now array'd.

Great nature's child can't christen'd be,
Of course not born in poverty.
Should prop of family but die,
The Church must get a chosen slice;
Of course the soul can't be switched off,
For century left on side track.
In purgatory's slums in pain,
Till wrong-doings for all are paid.
The very wicked when they leave
Across the Styx are ferried straight.
Glaun na ndoir, the other stream,
Purgatory across the way.
Oh, here the difficulty sure,
Unsettled bills are paid up, too.
A dozen masses smooth the way,
When a good price for them is paid.

The King of France in his heyday,
Fruit of his loins a bastard came.

He christen'd was without a doubt,
And royal sponsors, too, were found.
The kid became the conqueror great,
Of mighty Franco-Norman race;
His mighty barons, bastards most,
All church'd and christen'd and no hoax.

Way down the line, such is the case,
Dukes, lords, and earls, all the same.
Why even down to country squires,
Their bastards, yes, rate high in line.
Bastards of the later class;
Cadets, midshipmen, always rank.
But love-children of the common folks,
Poor slaves and tenants, nothing more.

It takes a pair to play a game,
Our royal team, the Church and State;
There is a team that can them match.
The double eagle Freedom's flag.
The issues that divide the pair,
As polar night to tropic day;
So circumscribed that neither yields
While lives a man a blade to wield.

They talk of days that tried men's souls,

A myth, a fable, nothing more.
The game accepted in those days,
Earth, heaven and hell contests the case.
The human race our property,
So says the State and big fat priests.
Freedom's sons alarm'd, forewarn'd;
The blow is struck, and dread the storm.

[*The Royal Camp. Characters,* WILLIAM, JOSEPH, HUM-
BERT.]

WILLIAM.

I'm of the mighty line of Charlemagne,
And none dispute—all, all accept the case.
His mighty power down to the present day,
Transcends the whole we next approach to same.
His feudal power, how vast the grand combine,
All western Europe, it the whole comprised.
That defeated Attila held the East at bay,
A feudal power is Germany today.

The human race, we must and shall possess—
Without the race the feudal game is dead.
This talk on freedom annoying unto me.
My men are free, as becomes men to be.
The freeman's life it is the soldier's trade,
And millions mine I count upon this day.

But this great uprising 'gainst our might to-day,
It must be down'd, though nine-tenths race were
  slain.

JOSEPH.

A Hapsburger, of ancient Roman fame,
Of royal line since Charles Martel's day,
Our subjects ever submissive to our sway;
But all is wrong, oh, yes, this many a day.
Science with our rule has interfered;
Against our might are several changes made.
Why, e'en respect—not none for many a day!
My supports are weak—I can't the point gainsay.
My best officers some time ago
Are not in this; their hearts elsewhere I own.
No fealty now to kingly state we find,
But, something mask'd, the devil lurks behind,
And what to do I really do not know,
For in our ranks our greatest, deadliest foes;
And to keep them from joining the other side
Our greatest efforts it will tax erewhile.

HUMBERT.

For to command respect and peace at home,
And hold at bay our enemies, also,
To hold the left flank—yes, against all odds—

Be it my duty, yes, and mine the task.
And should we fail upon this dreaded day,
My aerial fleet is ready without fail.
Success or victory, no middle way—
We must succeed, or perish in the fray.

At half-past five the battle is begun.
The terror, though, as the world's course was run,
Fifty miles in length and thirty wide,
As though the boundless ocean did ignite.
Who dare advance the struggle to retreat?
Who dare deploy the struggle everywhere?
But one great fact both parties do concede—
There's no advance! The fight is, to retreat, get
    away.

Armies now, as though the million slaves,
As the capitalists, had hold of lock and key.
It is so with armies upon this day,
As science now o'er human laws prevails.
A million men encamped on yonder plain,
An aerial scout the whole would sure stampede;
And ten such scouts would destroy the army whole.
Church and State, then cease to play the despot's
    role.

The mythology of prehistoric age,
The fairy legends of our youthful days,
The wildest fancy that the mind portrays,
More than verified upon this dreaded day.
God's chosen people—question, Who are they?
All ancient theories exploded on the case.
The eagle, greatest of the feathered race;
The man flies the highest to-day that leads.

At three o'clock the storm now is o'er,
The remaining scenes most harrowing to the soul;
For fifteen hundred square miles or thereabout,
Desolation, carnage, meets the eye all round.
The sport of kings was war in by-gone days—
If sport today, it is the people's game.
God's chosen temple folks, oh where are they?
Gabriel tooting, they're gone to hide away.

What dread commotion in the people's camp tonight!
At 1 A. M. the demons hove in sight;
The people looking for foul birds of night,
Were well prepared, and not at all surprised.
The lights of war are brilliant, no mistake,
And such exposed the monsters to their gaze.
'Tis now the upper shots that count, prevail,

And half the fleet, with crews dead, on the plain.

As quick as flash off starts the people's fleet,
Detailed for Italy, Austria, and Germany;
Their dreaded work, the world may calculate.
Poor, simple people, they wished to spare.
The Imperial Palace, many a ducal hall,
And feudal towers their destruction doth appal.
The blow was struck which made them sue for peace,
And Republicans rule o'er the globe today.

LINDEN HALL.

For three long weeks what pleasant days
In Linden Castle old and gray,
From war and strife some distance off,
Not e'en a courier with dispatch.
The pleasant walk in hazel shade,
For gods and goddesses fit retreat;
The dance by night, the party small,
A shade of sadness over all.

The good dame pondering on case,
Her lord and son both far away;
Dread war its chances calculates,
Which best or worst she cannot say.
Whichever party gains the day,

She prays to Heaven for their sake;
For Minister Reid her fervent prayers.
The hero that her castle saves.

The lovely lady Josephine,
A stranger yet to misery;
Of lovers she's got half a score.
This Yankee crowding in also.
But royal heroes are no more;
Republicans have swept the road,
And when the war is past and o'er,
The wind will point the course to go.

The terror of the battle's day,
All Europe trembled at the same,
And Linden Hall, not far away,
Our hero preparations made.
Flags and buntings he's got galore,
From outside wall to castle dome;
As peaceful frigate, in friendly port,
Her flags and bunting doth disport.

The war is over many a day;
In Linden Hall contentment reigns.
The marriage of our hero brave
With Josephine we celebrate.

Amongst the many guests are there
Scions of O'Donnells and O'Neills—
The kind, good acts of days gone by,
Why Linden towers still proud and high.

'Twas in September, as I remember;
The scene was Havre, that seaport gay,
The quarter-deck, our pair promenading,
The City of Paris that's underway.
With provincial lines now obliterated,
The age of science, reason, that doth prevail,
May war and clamor never mar the happiness
Of Charles Herndon and the Princess fair.

UN GAEL GO BRACH!

The ✠ Butler ✠ Campaign

IN MASSACHUSETTS.

Characters—B. F. Butler, Paddy Ford, D. Kearney.

CHAPTER I.

Patrick Ford and Augustine,
Teachers of men they claim to be;
To elevate the human race,
That of course their glorious game.
Twenty-one years ago to-night,
The *Irish World* saw the light,
First year *Don Quixote* came in shape,
Of course we knew 'twas boiler plate.
Following year *Arabian Nights*,
Prodigious, tremendous fine,
With his Mustapha, the tailor,
And Sinbad the sailor,
And the mighty Greek slaver
So lofty and high.

The Great Fords the teachers,
Denny Kearney the leader,
All professors and heroes
Are left far behind.
Ford a greenbacker uproarious,
That despised all cajolery,
That hated the bankers,
And syndicates despised.
He fought down the Harpers;
Jim Bennett he whack'd him,
And often he banter'd the Pope to a fight.
Sure, he teased the English,
Yes, and often most finish'd them;
The Anglo-Saxon's a myth,
In this last he was right.
He admires Denny Kearny.
And the Big Fours, he lauds them.
A holy penitent organ, his paper to-night.
He panders to the Mollies,
By the A. O. H. he's enchanted.
Industrial Liberator,
That's how he's self-styled;
But the parties liberated,
Like all such low creatures,

The far-famed liberator
They hate and despise,
For his actions have taught them
He's a fraud of the first water.
A bold Bohemian liner,
They claim he's to night.
General Grant's name is famous,
The admir'd of our nation,
The hero of heroes none will it deny:
Ford wrote the dictator,
An insolent shame 'twas,
Which meant for sale, I for sale am,
At a penny a *line*.
The great strike in London,
How immense the numbers
That defied the government
And bantered to fight.
Paddy Ford said the leader
Might rate as a hero
Less than Cardinal Manning or Kearney;
But Ford a shade higher,
As he furnishes the light.
Paddy Ford in politics,
As Don Quixote in battle,

Or as a donkey braying;
And that few heard the noise,
For the strings are too many
On his harp to handle.
He's nowhere he belongs;
A high private for life.

Now Denny Kearney of great fame,
That won renown upon the main,
A captain bold was brave Denny,
When he resolved to quit the sea;
To be a Jonah was his game,
Yes, or a Moses if you please.
'Twas musingly he thus had said:
I can and will reform the race.

My sympathy since a mere boy,
To aid degraded human kind;
To redress wrongs my studied care,
In this the hey-day of my days,
To ward off the oppressor's heel,
And to supply good will and cheer.
As best I can stop human woe,
This vale of bliss in lieu of woe.
The monsters that live on Nob Hill,

My business sure to curb their will.
The games that wicked men doth spring,
Such men and games will circumvent.
From now until the day I die,
Will elevate the human kind ,
And whether high or low in place,
My sympathy with the human race.
Now sand-lot meetings they were plann'd,
And Denny boldly chaw'd the rag
To hide-bound and priest-ridden slaves,
To fossilized chaws, demented knaves.
His oratory was well composed
Of slang of every foreign port,
And in sailor's boarding-house talk
Bold Denny was the lord of all.
Brave Moses led the Israelites,
For aught I know he made a point;
Peter, the hermit, stout and bold,
Impell'd to war crusaders bold;
But Kearny he outdone them both.
His line a ragamuffin' horde,
The scum of every race and clime,
And for a Big Four won the fight.
To recognize him now we know

Not even chaws from Erin's shore,
E'en such that for contractors work.
Of Kearney they have got enough,
E'en those for Carlo Mungo wait
They swear that Kearney is a cheat.
He's pension'd off—the case well-known,
For the work done for the Big Four.
Fortune smiled on brave Denny.
His bold heart throbb'd, the dame sang sweet.
How proud his hopes!   His heart beat high,
Not we to damp celestial joy,
Fear never sacred to the storm,
The smiles of fate portend no harm.
But heaven's frowns, all well aware,
The world's greatest must obey.
Favors, fortunes, are a lure,
And but the trials of brave and true;
A call to duty and no more.
The alarm gives, as foeman's note
Awakes us to the game of life.
For surely we must take a side;
For from the cradle to the grave,
All, all, they have their parts to play.
It is a dozen years ago,

For governor ran the Butler bold
In Massachusetts, classic state.
Amongst the noble and the great.
You read of Boston's fam'd city,
The Hub of earth, as all agree.
The classic Athens 'tis, also,
And mighty Troy was ne'er more bold.
O, here are ships from foreign climes,
Whose flaunting flags do sweep the skies.
Teuton and Celt, in friendly cheer,
Drink beer and thrive and flourish here.
The ancient natives of this state,
Of ancient British stock the same,
That freemen's laws always maintained,
Proud and high, a lordly race.
The Butlers are an ancient stock,
From commonwealth of Rome the fact.
Europe in the long ago
Oft quailed before the Butlers bold.
When Capet seized the crown of France,
The Butlers bold then led the van.
At Hasting's frightful bloody day,
In high command the Butlers there.
Seven hundred years on Erin's shore,

A shade 'neath royalty no more,
By Slany's banks and Barrow's side,
On stubborn Nore both proud and high,
Where many a field and fort and town
Doth cherish the Butler's fair renown,
And Butlers boast from earliest days,
In heart and soul of Irish race.
Politicians from away back.
The proud, the glorious Ormond stock.

When nomination Ben secured,
For spouters he was much confused.
Then musing he soliloquised:
This mighty game doth tax my mind,
My efforts now as ne'er before,
The Butler name for to uphold.
Against me now are all array'd
Of those the ancient British race;
The millions wrung from starving toil,
The starving votes will surely buy.
Of racial feeling not afraid,
I think on that about the same;
But they are educated, sure,
Their union will be fierce and true;
Their spouters all are silver-tongued

As though Elysian notes were sprung.
There is a hint at foreign race;
The natives they will tug and strain,
And B. F. Butler they will down,
If in the shadow of their power.
To swear and repeat, no chance here;
The stock are cunning, sharp and keen.

In several cities I've engaged
Spouters worthy of the name;
Irish and Americans, both
To me have pledged their proud support.
Could I this city but secure,
Then victory would be assured.
Now, here, a spouter I must have,
With foreign airs, whate'er the cost,
To thresh the air, sling foreign talk,
To grace historic Faneuil Hall—
One fill'd with vinegar and gall,
To make his mark upon the wall.
Pondering now upon this task,
Oh, where to find this man of mark!

New England cannot boast to-day
The man I'd honor with this place.

In New York no friendship there;
They hate and fear the Butler name,
And I despise the Tammany crowd—
A Butler still, both fierce and proud.
In San Francisco, on this day,
There is a man of talents rare,
In politics he's made his mark,
By smashing rings on the sand lots.
The Church and State he doth despise,
The Dems. and Reps. he does defy.
To elevate the human race,
It is his mission on this day.
I believe he's of the Celtic race,
Of Irish stock, both true and brave.
In affiliation, too, I know,
With those that to the seas do go;
He went to sea when a mere lad;
For several years before the mast;
To a captaincy he quickly rose.
The human race he leads on shore.
Could I this statesman but secure,
Opponents all he would confuse;
The banners in Faneuil Hall
Would dance enraptured on the wall;

His ringing speech in thunder tones
Would shake the knaves as ne'er before.
His burning eloquence in this place
The great Bay State with joy would quake.
Election day is drawing nigh,
Dallying time is just gone by;
To New York this day I go;
And destiny may interpose,
To point me out the righteous way
For to secure this statesman great,
To Frisco now no time to go.
A letter also would be slow,
He's lectured o'er and o'er the state,
The rings and cliques before him quail;
Spring Valley Water Company
No franchise gets from brave Denny.
They're a set of bilks, so Denny said,
To skin the crowd as other knaves.
On flood, on field, in foreign ports,
He's made his mark, aye, o'er and o'er,
The knaves have surely felt his weight,
In that the great, the Golden State;
Statutes, yes, and several laws,
He has revised them since last fall.

An emperor he's styled to-day,
I believe he's worthy of the name,
For he's done work as ne'er before.
Not on this fair Columbia's shore.
The mighty Hercules of old
He never, never, could do more.
The Augean stables he cleaned out,
And political pirates put to rout.

I'll take a stroll to Patrick Ford's—
A man of mark is Ford, we know,
A teacher he of men, also,
That ancient theories did explode.
In the labor ranks he pull'd an oar,
And rank'd a Jonah or a More.
His bearing this day proud and high
As Hector, fam'd at siege of Troy.
Nor Agamemnon in heyday,
That took command on Trojan plains,
The conquering hosts that down'd Troy,
Are naught to Paddy's well-taught boys.

[BUTLER *enters* PADDY'S *sanctum sanctorum, and the latter
salutes* BUTLER *in a half-civil, half-military style, but
in dead earnest as the editor of the Industrial Libera-*

tor, as a teacher of men, and as the renowned pointer of the administration.]

PADDY.

Thrice welcome thou, the Butler great,
From great Bay State, of classic fame.
Thy fame abroad those many days,
The Butler of illustrious race.
Charlemagne's history not complete,
Without the name of Butler great,
Agincourt and Cressy's plains,
Great Edward's power, they stemm'd those days
The barons bold of Brittany.
Their feudal power immense, supreme,
With Cœur d'Leon, in Palestine,
They won renown through blood and fire.
The Wars of Roses, too, so great,
The Butlers engineered the games:
At Ramilies and Fontenoy
On both sides Butler blades were high;
On Adda's banks, on Blenheim's plain,
With great Vendome 'gainst Prince Eugene.
Why, e'en in Erin, to this day
Without the Butlers naught is there.
Benjamin, of noble race,

Your visit here it doth much please;
Your commands here will be obey'd,
As fealty to the Butler name.
Proud Prince of the great Bay State,
And lofty branch of glorious race,
The earls fam'd of Ormond's side,
Their generous blood in you abides.
Your presence here, upon this day,
Infuses new blood into my veins;
To destiny I'm now resign'd,
My cup is full with bliss and joy.

[PADDY *fainted, he felt so good.*]

BUTLER.

My worthy friend and generous host,　·
Commands from me there's surely none.
I came to counsel to prepare
For the near, great eventful day.
I came not as a Butler bold—
A citizen's game is mine, no more—
To confab and confer with you
About the course I'm to pursue.
I've scann'd the case for all I know.
There's not along Atlantic's coast,
From Chicago to Mexic gulf,

A man, to-day, that I'd intrust
For spouter in Faneuil Hall—
Oh, that's Gibraltar of them all.
Scandinavians there in force;
Dago element's strong, also;
Portuguese cut a figure there;
Yes, and Basque's sons, from sunny Spain;
English, Scotch, and Irish, too.
The latter clan doth much confuse.
First Cork, then Connaught, 'pears to lead;
The bold Fardown, not much afraid,
And Orangemen— it is no hoax—
That whistle psalms to Willie's ghost.
When such the case, who would you name,
For Faneuil Hall, to clear the way?

FORD.
Now on this case for many days,
In sanctum here I prob'd with care.
The chances here of Os and Macs,
To pull an oar with Ormond stock.
Here Connacht men that's bold and true,
To pull an oar would go with you.
And Cork men oft that swept the road.
The kindred stock of Butler bold—

Of Fardowns, too, a chosen band,
The glorious stock of fam'd Red-hand.
With you they'd go to pull an oar,
As free as with the famed Hugh Roe;
But now the laws are so much changed—
No chance to swear, or to repeat;
No chance to bulldoze at the polls,
As in the good old days of yore.

Now where's the use in training men,
The government it steps right in;
Now where's the use to show the road,
The government our route ignores;
From here we cannot give no aid,
The facts are true and simply plain.
But were it as in days gone by,
We clear the way as Greeks at Troy.

Of spouters here I know not none
But of the common, common sort.
No Cicero or Demosthenes,
To rouse the world with their appeals.
No great Voltaire or Danton bold,
That down'd great states, empires threw o'er.
Such burning words as Winkelreid's

We'never, never hear such here;
Not even equal to O'Connell,
Or the grand old man Gladstone,
The low-lived chaws that cackle here.
Our oratory is waning fast,
The newspapers have got the start.
It's been supplanted, well we know,
By political pirates, game, bulldoze;
By stuffing boxes in job lots,
By throwing the same in sewer pots.
The machine and penitent gangs also,
Our oratory thrown overboard.
What's next the change I cannot say.
Election laws are strict to-day.

*er a lackey somewhat excited, who whispers something
into Paddy's ear.*]

PADDY.

A gleam of sunshine fires my soul,
Result of which we soon will know.
I know a spouter proud and bold,
That won renown in foreign ports.
The hero, yes, of several frays;
The marks are on his breast and face;
The redeemer of Pacific Coast,

Where rings and cliques gone overboard.
Oh this, the morning of his life,
What fierce foul work he's thrown aside.
My honor'd guest, you heard, I ween,
Of Kearney's fame the past two years.
Should we secure him, he's the man
To hold them down, the many clans
That muster will in Fanueil Hall
For to decide the governor's cause.

BUTLER.

I've slightly ponder'd on the same,
And oft have heard of Kearney's fame,
And, as the time is growing short,
Upon the same we better act.
Now telegraph without delay;
Find out if he can come this way.
His charges too, no after kicks,
I'm always square upon such biz.
Dear Mr. Ford, 'tis best we know,
The work to square as on we go.
The promise made and not fulfilled
Doth lead to many an after kick.
It entails misery and pain,

And lawyers harvest on the same.
Promises Ben never made,
And promises he'll never break.
'Tis home to Lowell now I go;
Attend to this the best you know,
And though I never promise make,
Life's record I will not disgrace.

FORD WIRES DENNY:

THE TELEGRAM.—Mr. Denis Kearney, Agitator and Reformer, City Hall, San Francisco, California:

Maker and Unmaker of men, I wish to secure your services for the Butler Campaign in Massachusetts. Said services will not extend beyond several lectures in Faneuil Hall, and two in Lowell. Wire at once, stating fees.

P. FORD.

KEARNEY'S TELEGRAM.

Message at hand. My fees will be five thousand dollars, to be paid to me on my arrival in New York; and in case of gaining the election, five thousand dollars more on my starting home.

KEARNEY.

FORD'S SECOND.

DEAR MR. KEARNEY—Creator of statesmen. Your terms accepted. Be prompt. Come at once.

KEARNEY.

Will start on the next train.

KEARNEY.

And have I lived to see this glorious day,
That with great Butler, I would take the lead.
Ten thousand dollars to me will be paid,
To lecture in the world-renown'd Bay state;
With such great strides my watchword now advances
I soon will ride the wonderful gray horse.
Nor check my reign though blood it flowed in streams
Till a minister I in distant far Cathay.

From prehistoric age, the facts well known,
Heroes in every age and clime well known.
In boyish days, my life, I own, was hard,
E'en down to that of life before the mast;
But such is history, all, all aware,
And destiny in grief and joy doth pay.
Upward and onward, 'tis fate now points the way,
Till a minister I in distant far Cathay.

Now this past century, how vast social throes,
And revolutions shook the world also,
Slavery's death this day doth celebrate,
And my record, too, how grand at Golden Gate.

There are some through life that take the backward
　　step,

And others, too, that fail for to progress.
Not such my style, as fate doth point my way,
Nor check my reign till a minister in Cathay.

[While *en route* to New York, his arrival was heralded at
the various points, and crowds assembled to see the
famous Emperor Denis, of sand-lot fame, of San Francisco, that had won political stars without number, and
now on his way to stump the great Bay State for Butler. The bulletin-boards announced the arrival and
departure of our hero. In Chicago he was captured by
admiring friends, and compelled to deliver one of his
irrepressibles to an enchained audience. Ford met
him at the depot, and brought him to his own house,
and welcomed him as though he was accompanied by
the daughter of the Son of the Sun.]

FORD.

Hail, gallant friend! A welcome here!
And for a week, a month, a year.
And on the spot your check I draw,
For it is Butler's high command.
Proud am I to see the day
That Faneuil Hall your presence grace.
Now should it be a victory,
With love and joy my heart would bleed.

My hero brave, this your heyday;
Oh, this the high noon of your days!
The blood that proudly held its own
Upon the wild Pacific slope,
Upon the stormy, wild sand-lots,
In Faneuil Hall 'twill soar aloft.
Your iron nerves and heart of steel
Will send opponents all to sleep.
Your nerves are strong, you've cheek and gall,
The best, the noblest stock of all.
In thunder tones your roaring voice,
All opposition it will quiet.
The Cape Cod element will quake;
The blue-blood stock will stand amazed.
When you do talk in Faneuil Hall,
The banners dance upon the wall.

KEARNEY.

Dear Mr. Ford, I'm very well aware
That yaps and mopes will often at me stare—
'Tis nature's law, we cannot call it more,
For dogs and cats look at the moon, also;
But what care I for low-lived blatherskites
Or Nob Hill bilks, that never mar my joy;

Among such stock, at home always am I
As the god-like Hector on the plains of Troy.

At San Jose, our heroes clear'd the way;
At old Gilroy, it was a similar case;
And in San Juan, the natives were amaz'd;
While at Monterey, we took and kept the cake.
In Boston fam'd, 'twill be a similar case.
The hearts of steel will give a welcome there,
With Dagos, Scans, and Portuguese, also,
And Butler stock to heaven itself will go.

On Boston heights, aristocrats live there,
With stripling scions, and simple blokes are they;
They're petted, nursed, brought up with tender care;
They'd never suit the Bruce or Douglass name.
'Tis other blokes that tantalize my mind,
That mislead thought, degrade all human kind.
The boys to me they will be true, I know;
Tó Heaven, by ——! proud Butler stock will soar.

Now, of my pedigree I feel proud and great;
With my turf life, the gods themselves are pleased.
No failure yet on the Pacific's slope;
And with God's help I'll straighten out these rogues.
Sure Agamemnon, at the siege of Troy,

5

He never wielded greater power than I;
With Cork and Connacht allied as of yore,
And Butler here, we'll soar as ne'er before.

[The meeting ended by the Industrial Liberator and the
great Political Agitator embracing tenderly.]

KEARNEY.

For centuries long the world o'errun with chaws,
To mislead thought, pervert all human laws;
Poor mankind bleeding in misery and woe.
'Tis fate! 'tis fate! so yell the fiendish rogues.
'Tis not fate, but work of cunning drones,
That's steer'd by knaves and cruel priests, also.
Why, upon my soul, I'll straighten out those chaws,
When Butler great doth regulate our laws.

We talk of Marathon and Thermopylæ,
Of Julius, Brutus, and of Roman thieves,
Of mighty Constantine that divided Rome,
Of Alaric that set Rome up also,
The prophet Mahomet of Moslem fame,
Of Moorish kings and mighty Charlemagne:
They were all a set of knaves, of bilks and blokes,
Though even great, Great Ben transcends the whole.

O'er Europe broad, through ages dark we know

The race was low, the tyrant's games their own;
What frightful wars to perpetuate their games,
Those born slaves as such they should remain.
What glorious times for royal Kings and Popes!
With long, sharp spurs the human race they rode.
With some the style until this very day,
But not the style with Butler's honor'd race.

In Boston now sometimes I there will stay,
And at the Clarendon will rusticate.
Here mighty grandees of the great Bay state
Doth spring great games on India and Cathay;
But those are bilks and simply frightful chaws,
And just as bad as sanctimonious frauds.
To degrade the race their dreaded game we know;
Their record ends when Butler clears the road.

In Faneuil Hall what thoughts will there awake,
And on its stage how proudly I'll sashay.
Human rights—my subject never old,
The Cape Cod bilks and chaws will soon be floor'd.
'Tis true Bill Coleman did my gang defeat;
But that is old, the scenes are far away.
With Ulster fam'd, with Cork and Connacht there,
Then clear the way, a Butler day 'twill be.

Kindred race, think of our island home,
No king was there since days of Conn we know,
They call'd them kings, as such they were not known;
The cards were play'd by sanctimonious Rome.
In Erin see the work of King and Pope;
Such dudes and chaws their games must be ignor'd.
To elevate the race our business is well-known.
With Butler's name and race high o'er the globe.

On Kearny's arrival in Boston a large number of the acquaintances of other days assembled to meet him, whilst others came through curiosity to see the distinguished stranger whose fame had preceded him. The sea-faring elements of the several nations were well represented.

The reason of their turnout is simply because there is a prophecy amongst them in effect as follows:

In the nineteenth century a seafaring man, and a reputed son of the god Neptune, would arise, and, after performing a number of political miracles, would then free the oppressed of all Europe. A peculiar feature of the case is that the strange being will be named Donoch Mungo by the Latins, and Donoch Carlo Mungoson by the Scandinavians. It is a well-known fact that the strange name in our language means Denis Kearney, and that accounts for the vast multitudes that attended the sand-lot demonstrations.

This very day Kearney is more potent in politics than his enemies give him credit for, owing to the fact that those people are as devoted to him as ever, even though their faith may be shaken as to him being the long-looked-for liberator. His admirers claim that facts were abundant to point him out, not only as a leader of men, but a man of destiny.

Butler called on Kearney at the Clarendon, invited him to his home and introduced him to his lady, who received our hero graciously and introduced him to her politician boy, between whom and our hero an animated conversation commenced, Kearney being the principal speaker:

Kearney.—" How old are you now, Jimmy ?" " Nineteen." " Going to school, I suppose ?" " Yes." " What are you studying ?" " The arts and sciences, metaphysics, psychology, etc., etc." " I'm quite astonished at your father to tolerate this nonsense. Jimmy, my boy, you'd learn more in roughing it through the Sierras, where you'd have a chance to study this Chinese rascality, and all over the Rocky mountains, just during two summer seasons; a couple of trips to Behring sea and the Aleuts, and a few trips to the South-sea islands. This is what would brighten you and show you your place among men.

" I never went to school, and if I do say it, no better navigator on any ocean or sea than your devoted friend, Captain D. Kearney.

" It is no bragging for me to say that I'm the political dictator of the whole Pacific Coast, and you can command my heart's blood, if I don't make Faneuil Hall shake, and all the knaves that will be there on next Thursday night.

" Call on me at the Clarendon, and I will show the blath-erskites and bilks there, as to who and what the youthful scion of the proud house of Ormond is and ought to be."

After several social passes, the proud Butlers concluded that the distinguished stranger was the professor of many political points.

The Meeting.

Faneuil Hall was crowded to its utmost capacity, all the nations of Europe being numerously represented. The meeting was further honored by many of the leading literary lights of Boston being on the stage.

Mr. President and gentlemen of the meeting—Being almost a stranger, it is but natural that you would like to know as to who I am and where I came from. Now rest assured that I'm none of the gutter-snipe breed, and it's immaterial to the case as to whether I was born in Clonmel or Boston. My father was a native of the devil's bit in the Shlieve bloom mountains, and mother was born on the south side of Shlieve ne mon. My two uncles, her brothers, took an active part in the battle of Carrig Shock, where sixteen peelers were killed.

Sergeant Wiley, the Orange ——, got away. A great army was sent out from Dublin to cut down the people. The latter rounded up the cattle of the county, with barrels of tar on hand to put on the cattle and set fire to them at the opportune moment, so as to break in on the artillery. The people had no generals, but they could get along well enough without. The great point was to get close enough to the soldiers.

Now, when the commander was forming his line of fight, and the soldiers were getting their cannon in position, Sir John, a nephew of the Earl of Ormond, rode up to the commander, and said:

" Look here, fellow, I'll just give you twenty minutes to get a move on your troops and a curve on yourself. We did not send for you, and we are running this part of the county for seven hundred years, and feel confident of our ability to manage an affair of much more magnitude than the accidental death of sixteen peelers. Of course it was accidental. They had no right to march in that Bohreen."

These simple peasants know nothing about war. The commander was the son of a Scotch or English lord, and afraid to tackle Butler.

You are all aware of the alacrity with which Ben would rein up a water-wheel or lariat a locomotive when employees were ill-treated—all going to show what is to be expected from the Butlers.

They will never disgrace the past. New Orleans was the cesspool of the nation, and Ben made it as clean as Boston. You cannot point to a solitary instance since Ben was in his teens where he refused to espouse the cause of the laboring man, the lonely widow or orphan, whenever there was the ghost of a show, simply because the Butlers are where they belong, and ever in sympathy with humanity.

I put it to a vote, so as to find the spirit of the meeting. All in favor of Butler signify by saying aye. [Aye, aye.] Contrary, no. [No.] There's but one no, and he's neither a bilk nor a blatherskite. He's some kind of a Darwinian that ought to be ashamed to sit among the respectable people of Boston. Gentlemen, should I be insulted by a galoot of this kind in Frisco, he'd hear something of it. Now, gentlemen, cheers for Butler. [Hip, hip, hurrah! hurrah! and again, in style never heard of before.]

THE CHINESE QUESTION.

Personally I have nothing against the Chinese, but combined capitalists, in their various workings and details, are the shining marks for my arrows.

Our ancestors at some time in the remote past came from the East, but God alone knows how long since. The round towers of old Erin have been built more than six thousand years. The ruins of Egypt and along the Bosphorus, still more ancient, were built by parties from the remote East.

We look toward the east for light. The sun rises in the east. The great heavenly bodies perform their revolutions in like manner. Emigration, as light, always travels from east to west, and for thousands of years it has been lashing itself to death, in Western Europe, as ocean's waves on a rock-bound coast. The Kingly Church and Masonic institutions, all from the East, but at what date? It never has been ascertained, but all ordinary scholars are conversant with the fact, that Europe was thickly inhabited. At the time of the *liaison* of the serpent and grandmother Eve, poor Adam hadn't the sand in him, so the serpent—his right name was Milo Gochrander—kicked them out of the ranch, when it suited.

For aught I know, we are of Chinese descent. Men of the heroic age wore queues—just imagine the fine queues worn by Hector and Achilles, at the siege of Troy. Two hundred and fifty years ago, in Cromwell's time, there was a law passed, prohibiting the Irish from wearing queues. It has been the custom of Britain's nobles to wear queues within the past century.

Patrick Power of Daragel, a noted duelist, that lived close to where I was born, wore two queues. As the beard is an ornament to the face, so is the queue an ornament to the head.   It is the genuine emblem of freedom, and I am very much astonished that our Boston dudes do not revive the custom.   But, gentlemen, it isn't in them; they're too fond of toadying to royalty and aping the nobility—a demented crowd that have pooled all their issues to down the brightest star on earth to-day—B. F. Butler.

[*The cheers within and without rent the heavens.   The wild uproar lasted fully fifteen minutes.*]

Money in Washington, to-day, coined in China seven thousand years ago.   Now, how many years previous has Chinese civilization existed?   I am frequently amused at reading little stories in the Bible.   No doubt whatever but, even in their heyday, the Jews were very low, and compared to the Greeks as a little penitent procession of New Mexico, carrying big crosses, would compare to a presidential procession in Washington.

I'm on to the Church Combination this many a day.   At present, as thousands of years ago, always dishing out the same kind of stuff to hold the multitude in ignorance and degradation—the support and footings of the various despotisms; and that is where we're at sea, as we do not know how does our candidate stand with the church sports, but we hope for the best.   And now, gentlemen, I appeal to all

here from within the limits of Cape St. Vincent and Arch-
angel, the Golden Horn and Donegal, and the great American element just as well, to cast aside all national jealous-
ies and feudalisms, and to join heart and hand, as the crusaders of old in the Holy Land, to pool your issues into one
grand common cause, and with a long pull, a strong pull,
and a pull together, rising in your might, as a great tidal
wave, and overtopping this Cape Cod aristocracy, and elect-
ing one of the grandest spirits on earth, B. F. Butler.

[Hip, hip, hurrah! The memory of the city of Boston will
be evergreen on the yelling and hurrahing.]

There would not be much objection to the Chinese coming
the old-fashioned overland route, to the west of Europe, and
then across the Atlantic to New York, but surely to God,
the founders of our mighty nation had no idea that the
countless millions of Asia would take advantage of the
clause, unrestricted emigration, and take the short cut across
the Pacific, swarming on our shores as the locusts in Egypt
or the grasshoppers in Kansas.

The moneyed power is in harmony with Chinese immigra-
tion, but when I get back to San Francisco I'll straighten
out the Chinese emigration, in style never to be forgotten

Here's to the election of Butler!—[Hip, hurrah, etc.]

Butler was defeated, but not through lack of oratory. If

any fault, 'twas too good, this being but a brief synopsis of one speech.

Butler said: "Oh, wisha, indeed, Mr. Kearney has injured me."

P. Ford to Butler.—"The dam'd old fool; we all knew that the importation of Kearney would have a tendency to unite opponents."

It was a spirited election, and Butler's supporters deserve more praise than censure.

CHAPTER II.

THE SPRING VALLEY WATER-WORKS, SAN FRANCISCO.

[*Scene in Platt's Hall—The People's Meeting*—PATRICK EGAN, *the first speaker.*]

GENTLEMEN AND CITIZENS—Since the world began we had cliques, rings, and syndicates, and it appears that our civilization cannot well dispense with them.

All our social evolutions, the making and unmaking of nations, races, and men; the changes of dynasties, kingdoms, and empires; rebellions and revolutions—all the work of cliques, rings, and syndicates.

The dreadful wars that have often almost denuded this earth of the human race; the suppression of the great

Knights Templar about the year thirteen hundred, thereby, as it were, making a present to the Turk of the best fourth of Europe; the retaining of the sultans and pachas, with their acres of wives—the work of syndicates, and principally of the Pope and kings.

[*A Voice.*—Mr. President, I rise to a point of order, and I'd like to know what religion and the Pope have to do with the Spring Valley Water Company. I claim that this is a Christian meeting, and that there's no necessity for the learned gentleman to go back to the wars of Troy so as to get a chance to punch the holy and blessed Pope under the ribs. Now, if he could make anything by it—but he can't; no, no, he can't make a speech of six lines in length without soaring away on infidelity. I know his game.

Voice.—Mr. Chairman, I rise to a point—

Chair.—Proceed. Egan said nothing to hurt the Pope nor nobody else. He wants to explain about the syndicate, and he's honest about it. He's not a heeler, nor a striker, nor a bulldozer for a syndicate or a big four. He wants to explain for the people the best he knows how.]

Egan.—Now Buckley is a heeler, always for syndicates of some kind or another. He's working now for the Big Four, and their little game is to bring water from Lake Tallyho, a distance of one hundred and fifty miles, and at a cost of one hundred and thirty million dollars. They are to bring it over mountains and through deep canyons, and under the waters of the bay. They can't do it; as soon as a diver goes down the sharks eat him.

The gang will furnish the money at exorbitant interest, and they'll take mortgages on everything along the line of route, from the lake to the city.

Should their little game pass, the people of a large portion of the state and city will find themselves blanketed and handicapped by a gang worse than the bishops and pashas that Egan was talking about.

As it has not escaped my practical experience, it is well to call your attention to their corps of civil engineers. I do not accuse all engineers as being scoundrels, but the majority can tell lies as gracefully as the preachers.

Now, I don't want to insult Buckley, nor anyone else, when I say that Rome leads in lying, and all the other little snide churches must come under the Roman whip. As we don't always see their rascality, we slight it, but engineers must get paid for their metric system and their strings of figures, and when it comes to add up, subtract, multiply and divide, they can do it from north to south, as well as from east to west. Gentlemen, they are hatching, but the birds of this nest will never be feathered.

[*A voice.*—Mr. Chairman, I rise. Gentlemen have been

vilified and slandered here unnecessarily. We concede that Mr. Herman Snyder is not playing the role of common heeler, but nevertheless he's a heavy stockholder in the Spring Valley Water Company. His brewery is of the larger class, and his residence is at present the headquarters of their chief engineer, the Baron von Humboldt. But as to the scoundrelism of the latter, we refrain from playing the role of critic, but Snyder has several little axes to grind.]

[*Cries of* EGAN! EGAN!]

Egan.—Gentlemen, I do not wish to trench on anybody's feelings, but parties that get insulted at a recitation of the cold facts of history, are so very sensitive that the whole social fabric can drag along without them. Without order I cannot speak.

The President.—We must have order.

Egan.—The greater the men the more powerful the ring. I will give but a point or two. At the time of the conquest of England, A. D. 1066, by the French, their pet name Normans, the syndicate consisted of the Pope of Rome, the King of France, and William, Duke of Normandy, the bastard son of the king. This syndicate had some backbone to it. The slaughter of the so-called Saxon race, a reproduction of the slaughterings by the Jews—all the work of God—ridiculous! Nothing in God's world but the work of the syndicate. The invasion of Ireland, A. D. 1172, the work of a syndicate. The parties to it, the King of France, the Pope of Rome and the King of England. The starving to death of several millions of the Irish in 1847, the work of a powerful syndicate. The Papal government got twenty million dollars for their work in the transaction; the money to be used in riveting the chains on Italy.

[*A dozen voices.*—Shut up, you s——. We did not come here to listen to any such string of lies. What do you know about history, as my——. Put your head in a sack and hide away. He's one of the kind that they raise in Ireland nowadays. I never saw it to fail yet, but when an Irishman or two or three of them want to start anything, a hound like him is bound to give it away. He can chaw purty fair, but no decent man could stomach such lies.]

[*The arrival of Mr. Picksley of the Argonaut being announced, he was warmly greeted by all hands. Being called on for a speech, he declined. However, he said :*]

I can tell on your dirty faces, that you never had a clean wash in your life. I can tell on your flabby jaws that you're beer swillers.

What's the matter with Egan? he's a fair talker, you pugnosed, long-ear'd herds. What do you know about a drink of good water? Your ignorance the best stock in trade of your owners. I never spoke of the orphanages of San Rafael and Los Angeles in public, but you are of that stock.

To make a speech for you and to commit suicide, the two last things that I would think of. You have scored another victory to-night, and might again for all I know.

Mr. President, I move that the meeting adjourn.

[At this time it was claimed by the opposition that the emperor Denis was sailing his boat a little too fly, and a few leading citizens held a private meeting with the object of holding a public meeting in the near future.]

Picksley.—"Should we hold another meeting, as they are the law, they are bound to break it up."

Du Nord.—"Kearney has been over-estimated as liberator. He's working for the Big Four. It and Kearney are the law, and there will be no protection for our meeting."

P. McNamara.—"Gentlemen, if in order, I'd like to pass a remark, in order. A well-known fact, that Mr. William Coleman has a proud record since the days of '56. I propose his appointment as champion, and as I might say, the guardian angel of our public meeting.

Mr. Von Hagan.—The motion is seconded. Carried unanimously that Coleman act as committee in general of the peace.

Chairman.—The meeting will be held at half past eight sharp, in Platt's Hall.

[*The scene changes to Kearney's Headquarters on Market street.*]

Kearney.—Our boys done very well at the meeting held by the chaws of Nob Hill. Yes, and they'll do better next time, as I'll be there myself to give them a point or two. 'Tis a shame and a disgrace, if we allow those fellows to bring their ditch through that part of the city, where poor laboring men have their homes.

[*A Voice*—It will be in pipes six feet deep.]

All the same, it will be detrimental to the prosperity of the city and the interests of the laboring class, and we have taken a stand, and will never allow it. The boys reined up Egan in the nick of time. It was from me he got his points. He was just going to come down flat-footed on the Big Four, the moneyed power, and their hoodoo games of aiding the Mugwumps of the East to start a monarchy here—China holding out her celestial arms encouraging 'em, and England, Germany and the Pope smiling at 'em. We'll hold 'em down, and don't you forget it! Picksley made the grand European tour lately, and paid his respects to the Eternal City by kissing the Pope's toe, and praising things in general there. I'm told he's Irish descent, but he only landed at Dublin, and went straight to Queenstown on the cars. And that's how the renegade

Irishman treated the loved island of the saints; and where but in Ireland would such miracles be performed as those at Knock, in a quiet glen, far from human habitation.

Picksley's business in Europe was a scheme bigger than even the Big Four dreamed of. It was a scheme to secure the consent of the Czar of all the Russias for the right of way of a railroad, from the mouth of the Volga to the frontier of China; distance, 1,792 miles.

He had a letter from the Russian minister at Washington to that effect, approved by the president and secretary. Does not this show on its facial mug as to who wants to sashay with and pander to crowned heads! Arrah, boys, but the Son of the Sun would have a fine chance to get rid of his surplus population. And it would have about the same effect on Europe as the deluge, or the rise in the Nile, or whatever they call it.

The czar gave him the duty shake.

Czar.—" Picksley, you go around to the other kings, and should they consent, I'll not kick."

Picksley.—" I want a recommendation."

Czar.—" Not much; you're a fine talker."

Now, gentlemen, that's the man; that's finding fault with the Lake Tally-ho enterprise.

Their game fell through, and the czar is to be thanked for saving Europe from a Mongolian inundation, that even the plagues of Egypt or the grasshoppers of Kansas pale into the small point of indistinctability when compared to it. He proved to be an ignominious failure amongst the Circassian beauties, and as a hobnobber among kings, and that's why his tirade against the glorious Queen Isabella and Catholic Spanish navigators.

He's even angry for the discovery of America; but what is to be expected of the far-down bloke. It won't do to abuse him, but we'll hold him down.

It is rumored that Coleman, of Vigilante fame, has locked horns with Picksley; he will find that '56 and '81 are different periods. He will learn that it would be more to his interest to attend to his hang-me-down business. If he could only see the one-eighth of an inch beyond the sharp point of his nose he could see how the six Chinese companies are doing him up, with Asiatic labor, at nominal cost.

Bill will wind himself up in the intricacies of his own net this very day. I cannot say a favorable word for him, except that in his youth, it looked, that he was a natural-born vigilante. Poor Bill.

Coleman was a heavy dry-goods importer, as well as being a hang-me-down merchant, and employed almost as many clerks as A. T. Stewart in his heydey.

[*The scene changes to the courtyard of Coleman's dry-goods store on Montgomery street.*]

Coleman to his Chief Bookkeeper.

"Can you do any carpenter work?" "Yes, some." "That's a block of mahogany, that was sent to me as a present from South America, and I want it sawed into the required length to make billies of, and as fast as will let you. Should you need a helper, call on one. The law prohibits the carrying of dangerous weapons. The billies are not rated as such. My boys must have something to defend themselves from the Kearney mob."

On the eve of the meeting Coleman issued a private call for volunteers, which was responded to with alacrity. The volunteers were ushered into a hall and there addressed by a gentleman in the flowing robes of a dominie. His eyes were small and piercing; his face clean shaved, except the mustache, which was black as coal and longer than any we ever saw on man or ——.

His Speech.

Gentlemen: I see a few here of the men that took an active part in the glorious days of '56. The spirit relegated to obscurity then is paramount and in power to-day. It is hoodooed, masked and cowed by Kearney and his men continually shouting the rights of the people. •

Now recollect that this is the moneyed age, and that the

Kearneyites are the cur-dogs of the capitalistic party. To-day the foul spirit and the law are one.

You are looked upon as the heroes of the people by the various races that have made San Francisco their home. Public demonstrations are necessary to the securing of the franchise, and I put the question, Did you come here fully intent to defend our meeting?

[*Answer, in murmurs low,* We did.]

The Kearney faction will be in force, and should there be any danger of our boys being worsted, the shout will be raised, '56 forever! You cannot stop in a cluster. You must spread out, with the intent of each making a circle for himself. Within ten minutes speaking will commence, and recollect that your lips must be sealed, and that nothing retards the feather of each arm.

You are looked upon as the bulwarks of the West, the champions of our civilization, of our people, and freedom, and we know and feel that every —— one of you will do his duty this blessed night.

CHAPTER III.

Coleman.

My arm has lost its vigor some, I own.
Yet head and hand are free to act, well known.

The present days are pleasing to my mind,
The type of those some time that have pass'd by.
In '56 we had some pleasant days.
Foul birds of night, they hop'd to run this place.
For them 'twere better their ambition not soar'd
Beyond the fields that knew their boyish sports.

Down on Meiggs' wharf a pleasant, bright May day,
A band of Thugs—with me they meant foul play.
Ned Graeme, a son of Scotia, lent his aid,
And o'er the dock a dozen Thugs went straight
Into the tide, unto the seething surf.
The whimpering curs! Right soon they cried enough.
'Twas but a joke upon their part, they claim'd.
In '56, then tough the jokes were played.
A hang-me-down merchant, I ne'er none;
From o'er the globe my goods came in shiploads.
A corner I on market never made;
The price went down when Coleman led the way.
Law and order I will still maintain,
By the ghosts of those that guard our homes in Clare.
Those prophets, leaders, and their scurvy hordes;
What care I for a Big Six or a Big Four?

Of lineage high, of proud and ancient race,

Antedating Greece or the Trojan name;
This day my kindred 'mongst the best in France;
In the British Empire still high their mark,
In the county Clare they are still in force,
In Chiquin, Adair, their county seats we know.
O'Briens, McNamaras, and the O'Deas,
Amongst my kindred still take their place.

Pool your issues, said Dinny, the chaw,
By the ghost of Conn, I'll break his Kerry jaw!
In this age of reason 'tis passing strange,
That silly Sthrapeens befog the race.
Such the games for centuries well 'tis known,
Such that play the music to the crowds also;
And this orpheus of silly slang and notes,
Is the filthy thing of our great Big Four.

A castle home in town of San Rafael,
Another such in Menlo Park to-day,
Fit to receive my kindred proud from France;
Or from fam'd Clare, should they but come along.
In Marin county my fam'd horse ranch,
In the mighty Comstock much mining stock.
All, all I'd give and a million more,
Before I'd submit to a Big Six or Big Four.

Emperor Denis has muster'd all his force
To burst our meeting—sure, the fact's well known.
Narrow-headed knaves and fossilized chaws
Will dictate rights and privileges, all.
Should that be so, I'll hide myself away,
And ne'er show up until a special day.
'Twill not be so, and believe now what I say,
For the boys I send go there to clear the way.

A few will be from far-fam'd Inishowen,
And two or three from glorious old Tyrone.
O'Connors will be represented there—
A section of the hall they will keep straight;
And Uncle Thady sends a good long score
From Carberry and Beara's rugged shores,
And Dan O'Keefe, a hero from Fermoy,
With kindred stock from town of Auchnacloy.
A few from Limerick and County Clare,
The Dalgais race—in van, in midst, and rear.

'Tis the poor, the lowly, the Poleen race,
Hurdy-gurdy element of Granuwaile;
The Irish magistrate blood-money pays,
'Tis such, to-day, that Kearny doth retain—
Such the dervishes and mamelukes likewise,

That many a day have enslav'd Erin's isle;
Here degraded creatures, foul, vile and low,
Drill'd for this purpose, and nothing more;
Their work is visible all o'er the globe—
The filthy flood will here go overboard.

[*The scene Platt's Hall, half past eight P. M.*]

First Speaker—I move that Mr. Heinrich act as tempo-
rary chairman.   Carried unanimously.

Mr. Heinrich—The first business is to elect a president.
I propose Picksley of the *Argonaut.*   Carried!   For Secretary, etc., etc.

Cries – O'Brien, O'Brien! etc., etc.

MR. PRESIDENT AND GENTLEMEN OF THE MEETING—It is
the language of our greatest poet that the greatest study of
mankind is man.

The leaders, the rulers, are meant.   This is the moneyed
age, and don't you forget it, and the man that's got the biggest pile is generally intrusted with the whip and spurs.
You've read of Venice, when it was a moneyed republic—
how vast its influence all over Europe.   The moneyed
power of Amsterdam, how potent in its time, and, like all
other forces when in power, what a dread tyrant!   The
United States to-day, the paradise of moneyed power.
The rings, cliques, and gangs of moneyed pirates in this

mighty nation are fearful to contemplate, and Frisco has a full quota of moneyed pirates; and who but a gang of such would ever dream of bringing water from Lake Tahoe to San Francisco?

This is not a myth, but a reality, as I'm well informed that engineers are perfecting the plans.

It is the mighty wealth of syndicates, or, in other words, organized piracy, that paves the way for royalty and imperialism. The Tahoe ditch is feasible. It is not necessary to pipe it 'neath the waters of the bay. It could come around by San Jose, and would be instrumental in founding an empire, duplicating to some extent the banks of the Nile in Egypt.

The people along its banks would be owned by the ditch company. It would be instrumental in creating the classes and the masses, and the many other ills that afflict the human race. We are not treating on the mythology of the prehistoric age, nor on the phantasies of fairy lore, as the scheme is far inside the limits of chance and probability.

And it further illustrates the fact that moneyed pirates, whether as individuals or syndicates, are to our form of government as the last stages of consumption to the human being—death.

A Voice.—Mr. President, I rise to a point of order. We

came to hear something about the ditch. What do we know about this nonsense?

" Why don't he talk about the ditch?"

" Ned is putting it on a little!"

" Note how long his ears are!"

As falls the hail on western plains,
Or fierce cyclone in Indian seas;
As river tearing through its banks,
Tame when compar'd to Coleman's bands.
Oh how the billies now were laid
On Kearney's gang with vengeance play'd,
A full round score insensible lay,
And peace again it reign'd supreme.

A Voice.—Mr. President, I propose that a vote be taken in regard to ascertaining the feeling of the people towards extending the franchise to the Spring Valley Water Company, etc., etc. Seconded.

President.—It is moved and seconded that all that's in favor of extending the franchise to the Spring Valley Water Company will signify by saying aye. [Aye, unanimous.] Contrary. [Not one.]

As the people and public sentiment are vindicated I move we adjourn. [Adjourned.]

Denis Kearney of great and mighty fame,
That won spurs and stars at the Golden Gate,
That proudly chaw'd and pranced on the sand-lots.
With the world's greatest he has hobnobb'd,
And with the bishop oft had a confab,
With commodores and admirals at home.
He captain once of Shooting Star well known
His too a case of weak and silly mind.
His fierce foul work the generous doth despise.
He fitting instrument of the Big Four,
To thresh the air and chaw the rag also.
As crop on crop, in Texas, horse thieves grow,
So shams and frauds of Kearny's kind also.
Both Denny and Co. sometimes have been unmask'd.
The silly toys that fate doth fling and toss.

A word to say about Spring Valley dam:
Since prehistoric age there's naught to match;
Not even Greece or Rome in their hey-day,
Nor in ruins of Pompeii, aught with it compares.
The shield of Achilles made in Heaven we know,
And even it, it was a shade below.
The docks of Liverpool are grand to-day,
And those of Belfast cut a figure rare.

Pigmy affairs—the work of Leprachauns,
That don't compare unto our dam at all,
But as work of savage of a bygone day,
To the skill'd mechanic of this glorious age.
Baron von Humboldt that drew out the plans,
Assisted by an engineer from France.

Cement, steel, marble as in molten mass,
By science placed regardless of the cost.
Here it is and here it will remain,
And Frisco's freedom it illustrates.
Its founders care not for Big Six or Four;
And Denny Kearney is thrown overboard.
And he's to-day of course, where he belongs,
With shams and frauds that long have been unmask'd.
For of all the wretches on this earth to-day,
Ford and Co. to lowest doth compare,
And Ford is one of a sham patriotic Four.
Inadequate am I to show them forth,
But a revolution such as Ninety-three,
And they the first should grace the guillotine.
The fierce, foul, poisonous, dread mistletoe,
Roots well-fasten'd in London and in Rome.
Horse-thieves in Texas the spontaneous growth;

But this a crop that never fails, we know.
Sham patriotism and Kearnyism also,
Sown with care fourteen hundred years ago.

Hurdygurdies in our cities promenade,
Degrade the Irish and the human race.
Those Asiatic games, that's very old,
Will be displaced by Freedom's games, we know.
The foul machine-unified vote to-day,
To degrade the race the cards that's ever play'd.

Oh where is Ford, not heard of him of late?
Between him and labor, deep the gulf today.
The Church has brought him the case, 'tis plain;
Put him on the shelf, where he will remain.
Dictator Grant, now the facts are plain,
The bold deserter that wrote the same;
The administration he overaw'd,
His mighty intellect surpassed them all.
Too big, too great, that's why he's been dropped off,
Still he gives points, and, careless of the cost.
Paddy, you of the silly, foolish games;
E'en in rhyme we'd scorn to give their name,
No notch to you in temple of great fame,
'Mongst the vile and lowly you're seen to-day.

Oh where is Butler of proud Ormond race,
The flower of chivalry, and of ancient name.
Of lineage high, almost kingly fame,
O'er Europe broad, theirs a lordly reign.
It makes no difference, mask on or off,
By their princely bearing, well known the stock.
Two thousand years, how proud the tide has roll'd,
This very day, a glorious stream also.
Right here is Ben upon this blessed day,
Peer of the Gods—who dare the point gainsay?
He with Bismarck wrestled, yes, and of late,
The Gaelic dog on top, you bet the case.
The Butler race, no silly toys of fate,
And though of earth, not easily brush'd away.
Oh grand their record on history's page,
A roaring flood their mighty tide to-day.

> William Coleman getting mellow,
> In the sear and yellow leaf;
> His circle, oh' how lofty,
> And he of it the chief;
> Since mighty Greece beleaguered Troy,
> Neither falsehood or disgrace,
> Upon his high, proud kindred
> Of glorious Dalgais race.

PICKSLEY.

I have made the European tour, and had letters to our ministers, but I never heard of the road to China before until I heard of it from the Kearny gang.

6

✠The✠Tramp's✠March✠

'Twas on a cold November night,
In North Platte town a tramp we spied,
And well beyond the prime of life;
But yet a man, tho' sad his plight.
His raiment, it was thin and old;
His tattered coat a tale unfolds.
He met two men, and of his name,
But not a whit for him they car'd;
Of course they were of Leinster stock,
And holy penitents, at that,
And Democrats, so they did boast.
Christian and Jew took in the whole,
But they were not from Cork, I think,
Nor Dalgais race from Inchiquin.
Now, where did he a dinner take?
A supper here he will not make,
Nor e'en a drop of Inishowen
To cheer his kind and generous soul.
No sympathy for him we find,

Nor friend with which to pass the night;
Now, in such shape, his lot is hard—
To face at night the winter's blast.
Mirza's vision, the bridge of life,
Upon it yet he proudly strides.
At nine o'clock the freight will start.
He hears the news with bounding heart;
So he crawl'd into a box-car,
To fight the elemental war.
His cat-naps on that dreary night,
Hunger, cold, his woes combin'd.
The following a pleasant day,
As o'er Wyoming sped the train.
'Tis here the cowboys gambol still,
But their wild sport was naught to him.
In four nights after him we find
Upon the continent's divide,
And switch'd off on the Sherman hill—
Oh, this, indeed, a woful fix.
Now, in an open cattle car,
The blizzard's blast there's naught to ward;
He yelled in terror and dismay,
Whilst fiercer still had blown the gale—
He curs'd and damn'd the Church of Rome.

And deem'd it cause of all his woe.
He cursed the Christian and the Jew,
Our civilization they abuse.
He cried aloud and wept betimes,
And deem'd it fate so reconciled.
Oh, how he danced that dreaded night!
Some humor in the dance likewise,
For well he knew that should he sleep,
He'd wake in death eternally.
Now, just before the break of day,
The stormy clouds had blown away.
The moon it shone both bright and clear,
As though a storm ne'er had been.
A house in distance now he spied;
With stiffen'd limbs right there he hied.
He kick'd the door, and yell'd aloud,
And very soon an entrance found;
And quick he lay down on the floor,
And soon his troubles all were o'er.
How sound, how happy was his sleep,
As though the angels fann'd his cheeks.
His dreams of times when he, a boy,
Done deeds that rated proud and high.
His dreams of men of other days,

And loving kindred passed away;
And little Fanny, his roan mare—
Glorious friends of her take care.
Then, raving incoherently,
Had rous'd the fair dame's sympathy;
For Con and Pat, her brothers brave,
Had been in frays and weather'd gales.
When he awoke it was near noon.
A bowl of punch the dame procur'd;
To him it tasted good and strong,
And rous'd the cockles of his heart.
A dinner also she prepar'd,
And fit for high prince of the Gael.
She paid his fare to Laramie plains,
Fam'd since General Harney's days.
A dollar, too, for luck-penny,
For well she knew its urgent need.
The dame a McNamara grand,
Of Dalgais race, from Thomand's land.
Her husband a conductor he,
And rated high amongst his peers.
Tramp will remember whilst he lives,
The lady fair at Sherman hill.
In a few days and him we find

At work, in great Ontario mine;
Situated in Wasatch range,
In far Utah, among the saints.
His wages three dollars a day;
For two short months how brief his stay.
The war is here, 'tis also there,
The cards of life they must be play'd.
The broils and strife of other days,
Are all aglow right here again.
Now there is none to aid the tramp,
And fearful now 'gainst him the odds;
Irish whisky-men, Christian knaves,
Hath sent him on the road again.
His clothes are good and strong likewise,
To suit the rigors of the clime.
Pondering now upon his route,
In this his grand mid-winter tour,
He cares not for the wintry blast,
Nor even blizzards, where they're hatched.
Should he take the southern line,
He'd winter pass in genial clime.
The brave and true will not retrace
The paths of youth and by-gone days.
Away, away, he northward hies,

To Montana's glades and mountains high,
Her towering forests, valleys wide,
And mines that beat the world beside.
In due time he arrived in Butte,
Its magnitude did him confuse.
He had seen mines in other times,
But only one Butte's prototype,
And that the great, the Comstock vein,
Virginia City in heyday.
But here no friend our tramp had found,
The smell was strong from all around.
There's nought on earth with it compares;
Possibly it's a duplicate
Of cities burn'd on the plains
In leprous Jewish bible days.
He's now cut loose from the railroad
And packing his bed all the go.   .
He's traveled many weary miles,
But no work our poor tramp can find.
At Blue-eyed Nellie stopped some time,
A rich and famous silver mine;
The property 'tis of the Browns,
Americans of fair renown.
He's heading still for the cold north;

The wintry blast it little mars,
And when he reach'd the N. P. Road
Toss'd up to find which course to go.
The West has won, he's gone that way,
To Puget's sound, Pacific's wave.
Though money gone admits the fact,
He proudly strolls on Puget Sound.
Four times he's made the full grand round,
From Honey Glade to Puget Sound.
War to-day on laboring men
Beyond his ken, don't comprehend.
Capitalistic whip the tool;
The hellish Jew directs its use.
The Jew forgets past chivalry,
And feats of Norman dentistry,
Pulling Jews' teeth in bygone days—
It paid immense to those engaged.
'Twas labor founded Greece and Troy,
And commonwealth of Rome likewise.
'Twas labor grand in Alaric's days,
That set foul Rome in mighty blaze.
It is one hundred years ago
Since from its sleep it then arose;
The Inquisition and Bastile

It sent to hell in smithereens.
The pet empire of foul Rome
Passed in its checks to rise no more.
From this great nation debt is due
To mighty labor, not to Jews.
As well attempt to stop the wind
As put down labor unified;
As well attempt to stop the tide
As down the mighty march of mind.
The Latin tide how weak to-day,
For so the Jewish Solons claim,
For they want kings and senates, too,
And Jewish blood for to infuse
The filthy, foul and leprous tide.
A use for it none dare deny,
To furnish gold for war and strife,
To kill, to murder and despoil.
How proud their boast, the Jews to-day;
Foul, vile in every clime and age.
Birds of night eagles might assail.
How loud the prude of Billingsgate,
The mule that's got no pedigree
How strong and high he kicks his heels;
Just see him kick, and prance, and bray;

For pedigree what does he care?
Now it is so with thieving Jew,
His pedigree just like the mule,
If otherwise, not then no need
Of circumcision foul and mean.
As cattle-thieves how short your reign;
With sheep and goats 'twas just the same.
As grangers you were very low,
And down to Egypt slaves did go.
Your history a filthy stink,
No other nation low as it.
Holy Writ your history call'd—
Siwash Indian o'ertops it all.
Filthy prototype of cuckoo,
Or he your prototype—no choice.
Foul destroyer of human race,
Not you o'er us to hold the reins.
On Waterloo's eventful day,
A golden harvest you made there.
The bible prates of fishermen;
Both prince and beggar fill your net.
To your dread greed naught that compares
But buzzards, sharks, and monsters rare.
Many a cowboy Jew's array'd,

With prancing steed, in burnished mail,
For glorious war in Holy Land
Between the Crescent and the Cross.
Oh, small the odds which gain'd the day;
The route to heaven the stake at play.
Principal and interest lost
By holy Jews, the case too bad.
The Norman race not dead to-day—
When was it so? the question fair. .
The iron race of Normandy,
The dreaded scourge of Jewish thieves.
Kings and dukes leprous to-day,
A prophet needed them to heal.
The crop is ripe this many a day.
The leprous horde must emigrate.
There's royal Vic., of Jack Brown fame;
The Argyle crowd are just the same.
Demented lords and leprous dukes
Affiliate with filthy Jews.
Oh, where the mighty, Strongbow race,
The princely, proud, the fam'd DeClare?
Pulling Jew's teeth he made his raise—
History oft doth state the case—
To raise the gold to give Brian Roe,

To start a ranch on Shannon's shore.
The Geraldines, both proud and high,
The Butlers bold from Ormond's side,
The ancient stock are still in force.
Ever renown'd the Macs and Os.
What! such submit to Jewish sway!
And cheese the moon, the case the same.
When our John L. to Congress goes,
'Twill be his biz, we all do know,
To have the bill prepar'd with care,
That labor travels just as freight.
And other members, firm and true,
Will here aid in passing through.
It is meet work for hero brave—
Then bless'd the name Sullivan bears.

THE DEDICATION

GATHOLIG ✠ UNIVERSITY

WASHINGTON, D. C.

NOVEMBER 11, 1889.

[*The curtain goes up, and discovers a few members of the great Catholic families of America, the great Jewish bankers,* BELMONT *and* SELIGMAN, *and nine of the leading Mugwumps of New York.*]

A whisper amongst them: "Our sons that graduate here will be on the plane of equality with the nobility of Europe. Ah! that's the scheme."

[*Enter the Cardinal,* ·ANTONELLI.]

You all have read of Charles Martel's fame,
Of Franks and Huns in dread and fierce array,

Of Charlemagne, his mighty glorious reign;
The grandeur, prestige of our glorious race;
Of Urban the Second, the good and great;
Of Henry the Second, in history fam'd;
Of Nellie Oge, the Queen of Aquitaine;
Of our power and strength, to last while time re-
    mains.

The Crusade wars will live on history's page,
So will the valor of our heroes great,
The blood in rivers for the cross that flow'd.
Oh, green their memory till time's no more;
Upon the sands of Afric's torrid shores,
In Palestine, what millions lay in gore—
Three hundred years—what dreadful carnage there!
The cross triumph'd, till time's no more the case.

Here a glorious empire, on this blessed day;
On history's page there's naught to it compares.
With South America, so grand and great,
For outlying provinces, what a picture fair;
As mighty Rome, in days long, long ago,
Her outlying provinces her strength support—
The world at large to pay tribute to our throne,
And heaven itself will smile upon the whole.

[*Enter* Col. McCoy, *one of the F. F. K.'s.*] This regiment
took a vote on the unpleasantness. So colonel and regiment joined the fortunes of Uncle Sam. Of course he's
a Democrat, but the teachings of the Fathers and
American ascendency his gentle racket.]

In classic halls I spent my early days
In Valladolid, yes, and Notre Dame.
On my plastic mind they failed to impress make;
Impressions here are those from Henry Clay.
The dreaded contrast still appalls my mind;
Ours the tropic twilight, theirs the polar night.
Now where in history can they other show,
Than rape, robbing, plundering, misery and woe.

Since freedom on this earth assumed control,
Here the sunshine of progress as ne'er before;
Here inspired thoughts, awakenings of the mind,
For thousands years such pictures you can't find.
Our phonographs, our telegraphs, also,
Our railroads too, our palaces afloat,
To navigate the air the day not far,
And heaven itself drags our triumphal car.

From Constantine's until fam'd Alaric's day,
Just eighty years were wedded Church and State;

The term short, in history's page a void,
To give details nauseating to my mind.
A. D. four hundred and fifty, mighty Alaric came,
And Roman glory, since then on the wane.
Your outlying provinces, such we contemplate,
New Mexico and old Erin, oh what duplicates!

Supreme power!   Omnipotent, all own!
And you pretend, of course, to know the whole.
You championing God! a horrid blasphemy;
Your implements of torture make the senses reel.
To kill, to make kings and nations, your dread game;
E'en though as billows were heap'd the slain.
Our nation's martyrs point to your work to-day,
Our great and small all well aware of case.

Your progress on immortal car of time,
Dread human monsters point to the head line.
Psychology the doctrine of the soul,
For human ills it covers up the whole.
Pack saddles for donkeys in New Mexico;
Enterprise there, how dismal is the show.
To give details unpleasing to my mind,
The mantle of charity covers all from sight.

Oh Roman poets brag with martial joy,

Of the Sabine days, when virgins they defiled;
Of your founders, suckled by the wild beasts,
Of the blood and carnage of your early days,
Of the Romans' glory, of their chivalry,
Of the Roman disk the Roman arm wields.
Oh the filthy pictures, just the same to-day;
On Hennessy's murderers, poets sing their praise.

On their feudal castles, with their donjon towers,
Oft peasants hung from trees that grew around.
Of the hoary abbeys and the college gray;
Of the classical ruffians, there did vegetate;
Of the peasant's wife, his blooming daughter fair,
Of ruffians' lust on such for to appease;
Of dreaded ignorance, your foul stock in trade,
On history's page nought else to duplicate.

The biggest ruffians upon the globe,
You canonize such, upon my soul.
To turn the coat with you an honor great,
Except it be with low and hide-bound slaves;
But should these from the traces cut and run,
With rage and hate, the fiery cross is sprung.
Your sentence reads, to fields of dread sheol—
The fumes of Butte doth surely point the road.

No sympathy ever with human race;
To hold them down, oh, that's the classic game.
To pervert nature, your studied law,
And cunning knaves to put on top of all.
Our glorious progress on this blessed day
It breaks your heart to follow far in wake.
The games that suit the very clime and zone,
The whole are play'd, the light excludes the whole.

In Alaric's days you did evacuate
The British Isle; it was decreed by fate,
Where'er the saint had learned the Irish tongue,
"Twas through that means the hellish work was done
As age on age doth come the social change,
And central power since then was banish'd from
    there,
A nation's regiment, a frigate not known,
Not since to sail from my own loved island home.

Our glorious Sunburst never knew defeat;
With Neill and Con o'er Europe oft it blaz'd.
Our fiery cross at night the signal flew,
And but one clan our glorious isle then knew.
A girl's picture playing a fiddle to-day,
A hound-pup to raise the martial strain,

The bunch of clover, the myth it personates,
Slavery's emblems—none dispute the case.

Monopolists, a curse upon this day,
And well it's known how long you led the race
To smother light, to crush awakened thoughts;
And that well known, the dreaded game of all—
Your editors all o'er the globe, a host
To polish foul and filthy lying notes.
Grade 'neath grade—oh, many the entails
To degrade the race, to grace imperial state.

[CARDINAL MAZARIN, *at dedication of University.*]
To hoodoo nations, either night or day,
And titled nobility for to create;
Manufacture slaves, degrade human race,
Classes and masses to regulate;
We teach God on high, Holy Church, also—
A mighty nation, just as ancient Rome;
We hoodoo nations, people agitate;
The key, the product of our ancient games.

Divide and conquer, Cæsar's shout of yore;
Our method, best of all, was tried or known.
Now, where a king, a half dozen we create;
And where a duke, we make a score, at least.

Here mighty war cannot much interfere,
The title lives, result of field what may.
Now Germany, her long eventful days;
Our patent's good none dare the same gainsay.

The Celtic race, and of the British Isles,
Oh, how we hoodoo'd them Europe doth admire.
They were a bold, proud and lordly race;
They will not unite, no, not while we remain;
The devil, of course, we credit with the mark.
The mystery they never care to solve.
Their ownership, it is no shabby boast;
They the greatest property upon the globe.

Should we come here, and let us hold the lines,
At this mighty nation, the heavens would smile;
A hoodlum race here, as in ancient Rome,
To scourge the world, and our laws enforce.
From Puget Sound and the Golden Gate,
We'd hold Japan; yes, and far Cathay.
The disinherited of the British Isles—
A hundredfold the race would soon enjoy.

The disruption of Roman Empire No. 3,
A telling point, the world on that agrees.
War's wild commotion, Freedom's cannon's roar,

Would imperil our rights we freely own.|
They're ours by weary centuries of entail;
Our temporal and spiritual props are they,
And blood in rivers will surely flow
Ere we relinquish on them our hold.

O'er Japan, India and far Cathay
Our hoodoo games I fear will not prevail.
Our mighty power on flood and field to-day
O'ershades the East in terror and dismay,
When such the case for hoodoo games no call.
Might is right, we wear the crown of Mars;
The Turk is dying, the East is on the wane;
O'er the demented Orient we hold the reins.

Dillon and O'Brien will be handicapped,
And our archbishops they will toe the mark.
Ere long 'twill be a contested case
As to who amongst the Irish will prevail.
'Tis fourteen hundred and fifty years
Since Irish kings unto us bent the knee;
From then till now they did not even dare
To be other than a low, a hoodooed race.

Dillon and O'Brien, both are renegades,
And against them issued our fierce mandates.

Papal property the Irish, the fact's well known;
Our imperial rights, they cannot be ignor'd.
Their land league rights, their silly canting talk;
Our will their rights, we dictate law and cause.
It has been so since days of Cromwell known,
And will be so while lives a holy Pope.

Religion, most truly it we teach;
Discipline, too, to govern human race.
Born free and equal, it we do ignore.
It never so, nor will till time's no more.
The master born—yes, and so the slave.
It's ever so, and will while time remains.
Our demand is just: with you we claim control.
The world itself to you we will bestow.

Hastings' slaughter, what a dreaded day!
'Twas mighty Rome that engineered the games.
Seventy thousand Saxons when commenced the fray,
A corporal's guard, about, what got away.
Saxon civilization very low,
A solid fact, which all the world will own.
At our behest a mighty nation grew.
The sun ne'er sets on its domains, 'tis true.

You, younger branch of our glorious race,

From west of Europe,˙all admit the case.
You, not of mushroom growth all, all aware;
The younger branch of mighty Rome the same.
All Europe points with pride upon this day
To this mighty stripling of the Celtic race.
Here we are, and with you we'll remain,
Whether or no with you to hold the reins.

How grand and imposing, all o'er the globe,
Our spacious palaces, their princely domes,
Our universities, our abbeys gray,
The true index to our state and grace.
This continent ours, our rights precede all claims.
In joint stock co. we love to steer the games.
Your precedence all o'er the globe, no fail,
And politics the mighty cards we play.

[It being arranged that Blaine was to reply to the distinguished stranger, and he being in a state of physical per-
spiration, his friends supposed that it was through fear.
Col. Butler, a Kentuckian, slapping Blaine on the should-
er, said: "Hold up your head, Jim. Don't be afraid of that
furriner. I'll see you through, and stay with you, and don't
you forget it."]

BLAINE.

To sectarianism I have nought to say,
Our constitution in it yet no change;
It's hoodoo, hoodoo here, your steady game,
And blind are those that cannot see the same.
With boodlers you never find no fault,
They're the elite and that amends for all;
Your work is foul—at least unto our mind,
And not for such we'd change our laws divine.

Now see them marching, how foreign to our laws;
Halt, right, gee-woh, the games are known abroad
The fierce unification of a hoodoo'd race,
The hoodoo'd votes, that now decide the case.
The noble American reigns here today,
The noble Roman figures small the case.
Then come what will, with you we'll have no deal
Historic marks, we shudder at the same.

Some time ago you hoisted Irish flag,
On city hall in City of New York.
Now when had the Irish a nation's flag?
If history's right not since the days of Conn.
They had hoodoo penitent flags galore;
Penitent kings without respect at home.

A nation's emblem not since there known,
Nor wont while classic hoodlums man the boat.

It was call'd a victory for the Church 'twas claim'd,
But the Sabine heroes it would disgrace.
At the heart of the nation now you make a drive,
E'en such a victory you will not enjoy.
The days of hoodooing are long past away.
The nation's longing for the coming change.
Mind, reason, science free upon this day,
The reason why hoodooing's on the wane.

Roman Empire three pulls a heavy oar.
Hoodlum stock the case it is well known.
A chain of arsenals around the globe;
And mighty fleets that's mann'd with hearts of oak.
Our nation's energy doth run that way.
We must prepare for coming storm, 'tis plain.
A good torpedo boat or device rare,
Were worth a million years of canting prayer.

Impossible for you to change your game;
Imperial, you will and must dictate;
Why even here precedence you doth take,
And draw the mark before the cards are play'd.
This ponderous pile doth not suit here to-day,

A use for it as other things that's made,
To polish dudes and Mugwumps, case 'tis plain,
To send to toady, to court of St. James.

The Cleveland factions are well known to-day,
North of the line in sympathy 'tis plain.
Canadians pray with all their might and mind
That such as Cleveland always hold the lines.
The nation then would become passive, quiet;
Then Britons bold could hector as they like'd;
Then at Behring Sea, or coast of Labrador,
A Yankee captain dare not blow his nose.

Language is given for to hide our thoughts,
But religion the darkest cloak of all.
Now where on earth can you any find?
'Tis just a guy for sickly weakling minds.
With Cleveland you run in harmony,
And Buffalo Bill states he's of that creed.
There are others here to be spar'd we find,
As the floating driftwood, who cares to mind.

Empire three your favorite, none gainsay;
It has been so since Waterloo's dread day,
And with the vengeance of a Tamerlane,
For her sake a continent you'd depopulate;

You have done it oft, then why not again,
As the tide doth history itself repeat.
Ancient Britons and Celts this earth dominate,
And with God's help, till time's no more the same.

As hoodoos, thugs, duffers, your pets first known;
Saloon graduate statesmen they next bloom forth.
Saloons they own, and others they control,
As noble aldermen, they graceful pose.
Their business now towering very high,
As undertakers how they cut a e   .
Socrates, Demosthenes, intellect overflows;
To Congress now the hoodlum hoodoos go.

Here noted statesmen play their hoodoo games,
And, at their death, what little that remains.
By hoodoo'd votes they grace our Congress halls—
Manifestations, immensity of gall,
In this age of reason, the picture plain.
The foreign hoodlums here will not prevail;
Here reproductions and revampings quaint,
Away far back the first duplicate.

All over Asia, during heroic age,
Gods and goddesses on earth then reigned.
As Irish kings—oh, yes, or highland chiefs—

The gods themselves, in pleasure, dwelt in Greece.
Why, of course they hoodooed in those ancient days,
And, to this day, 'tis a continued case.
But, as appearances doth indicate,
The game will fail in Uncle Sam's domain.

Classical, scientific education high,
To degrade the race the work of studious minds.
From high they get the pointers, so they claim,
To keep manufacturing the million's slaves.
Their horrid work, how dread to contemplate;
The devil, sure on him they lay the blame.
By slaves begot, as such you do remain,
But foreign hoodlums here will not prevail.

The silly psalms, the shouts are getting quaint.
Across the Styx, you'll go to Heaven straight.
The sum and substance of your ancient games;
It is here to hoodoo our good and great.
Your hoodlums here to-day are getting bold;
Your boodlers, too; of course you claim the whole.
You had the run, the world aware we find;
We prefer Greece, aye, e'en the games of Troy.

A poor fallen woman could be brought to shame;
Your shame and conscience no contrast we make;

Your dreaded schooling makes you monstrous vile.
Your horrid work murdering human kind.
Now where in history is aught to show
Of Comus breed but murderers vile and low,
When poor bleeding nature from her sleep doth rise,
Across the Styx you'll speed'ly take your flight.

Here's to the fathers of this nation great,
To the glorious intellects that's here to-day;
To Mars and Minerva our patron saints
That ever did despise a hoodooed race.
To the illustrious, the good and great,
That human rights always maintained explained,
To the coming struggle all o'er the globe,
To foreign hoodlums their overthrow.

CAPT. O'CONNOR.

Air—"Cove Harbor."

Now here's to the Golden Gate,
To the glorious city by the sea;
To 'Frisco's hoodlums stout and bold.
To found an empire such as Rome,
The Sabine games will be ignor'd,
As they'll have women of their own;
And surely not since siege of Troy

None to match 'Frisco's hoodlum boys.

Who cares for breed of Charlemagne
Or the Southern Bourbons just the same?
The nigger 'neath the southern lash,
Hoodooed whites no higher rank.
But here's to the good and great
That dared our rights them to explain.
To the true, the generous and the bold,
That Asia's fogy games ignore.

Oh, here's to Harrison and Blaine,
Of the glorious, ancient British race.
Here's to the glorious Celtic race—
To-day this earth it dominates.
The hoodlum games of the cursed past,
We know them to our bitter cost.
The ancient grafts are here ignor'd,
To the true and great our best support.

From Hudson's bay and Labrador,
To Terra del Fuego's shor
The joyful news we'll soon proclaim,
One tongue, one flag will grace the same
Here's to the brotherhoo of man,
To the glorious spirits of this land,

To the true, the generous, and the great,
To those that hold the reins of state.

FELIX McGUIRE.

Before psalm-singing commenced in these isles,
Here the homes of the mighty and free,
Invasion to Erin then unknown,
And Scotia well championed, I ween.

In numbers not over a score;
Naught o'er Europe to check our career.
We were victors where'er we'd abide—
Yes, and conquerors wherever we'd be.

Generals we furnish'd to Spain,
Whilst o'er France, then, we done as we pleas'd;
Our tribute came over the main,
Whilst the Greeks sang the praise of our chiefs.

Long centuries, no nation, 'tis plain—
'Tis Cæsar's cursed maxims that's here;
Long centuries we're hoodoo'd, 'tis plain,
The woe of dear Gra gal machree.

Should we but unite, say the knaves,
Our masters would flee in great spew;
Oh, Comus, and your monsters foul,
The dread curse of Gra gal machree.

Long centuries these penitents doth march
And clans to each other that's fierce;
On each other we fasten the chains;
By classic hoodlums hoodoo'd are we.

As the sun it doth rise in the east,
In the east so will bugles first blare;
How rivers of blood will be shed,
With terror the earth it will quail.

How science has lately advanced,
With wonder on each feature we gaze.
It looks as the work of the gods,
All dread evolution and change.

But better the tempests of war,
Than to slavery to have us consign'd.
Long have monsters polluted the earth;
Then to Mars we our chances resign.

Success to America and France,
The homes of the brave and the free;
We've hoodlums enough of our own,
And here's Freedom to Gra gal machree.

UN GAEL GO BRACH.